Destiny

Destiny

Book One of The Academy Series

D. D. LARSEN

Copyright 2021 D. D. Larsen

All rights reserved. No part of this book may be used or reproduced by any means, graphic, electronic, mechanical, photocopying, recording, taping or by any other means, unless given written permission from the author, except in case of brief quotations used in articles and reviews. This is a work of fiction. Names, places, and characters are used fictiously and not based on actual events and people.

ISBN: 9798590496785

For all those that need a push to follow their dreams.

Chapter 1:

June 1, 2020

Adam Ford
Senior Research Manager
Amtika
1480 17th St.
Denver, CO 80204

Dear Mr. Ford,

I would like to notify you that I am resigning from my position as Research Assistant for Amtika, effective June 15, 2020.

Thank you very much for the opportunity you've given me to learn all about pharmaceutical research and new age biological technology. I have genuinely enjoyed my time with the company, and

I believe the experience has taught me important skills and given me insight into the industry.

This will be my official notice. I will be around to assist in any way I can until I leave.

Best Regards,
Jamie Carter

I press send on the email, lean back in my chair, and take a deep breath.

My dream-job-turned-nightmare is over.

Since graduation, my path has been lined with mistake after mistake. I need some time back home to get my mind straight.

My apartment is packed, and everything is shoved into the new Subaru Crosstrek I bought last year when everything was still looking so hopeful. All I ever wanted to do was be successful, put in the work, and make my way to the top. Escape my small town.

But I've blown it. Big-time.

As I get on the highway to make the hour drive to the small town where I grew up, the tears start to fall. I have failed and it's all my fault. I'm not even twenty-six, and I feel as if my life is ruined. The hole I have dug myself feels inescapable. This mistake is only my most recent mistake of many.

I left home because I felt trapped. My hometown has its

claws deeper into me then I realized. As the life I have built over the last seven years crumbles around me, my childhood town seems to call me back by promising comfort. I just hope I will be welcomed back after the way I left.

My tears slowly dry up as the familiar scenery of home surrounds me. My heart comforted by the familiar beauty of the mountains. But not enough. I'm back, but more lost than ever.

Chapter Two:

Three years ago, when I landed the job as Executive Assistant to the CEO of Amtika right out of college, I was ecstatic. My college friends weren't having much luck, yet I had accepted a good job with one of the top biotech companies in Colorado, offering a lot of opportunity. It was everything I was looking for in my first job. With my salary, I was able to rent an apartment in the city and walk to work every day. I'd made it. The hard work had finally paid off.

Then, I did something stupid.

I slept with my boss. He made me feel special; he made me feel different—until we got caught in his office. To save face, I got transferred to the research department. This move was in the direction I had original hoped to progress, but it felt like a punishment, not a promotion. And I got dumped, or more like ghosted.

I had never planned on being an executive assistant. With my Chemistry Degree, I'd planned to work in research, discover the next cure for cancer, or discover something groundbreaking to help save lives. But all the entry level jobs I looked at wanted five years' experience, which seemed like a total oxymoron.

During my job search, the Executive Assistant position opened up, and I figured it couldn't hurt to apply. Somehow, I got it, even though I didn't have much of a resumé. I was so happy to be part of such a well-known company. I figured it was a stepping stone, since everyone always says that once you are in the company, it is easier to move around to a new positions.

From day one, I took the job seriously. I'm a very organized person; lists and color coding has always been my go-to for keeping things straight. My boss, Mr. White, was busy; always traveling and rarely stepping foot into the office.

I didn't meet him for three months. All our correspondences had been done through email. When he walked in the first time, I recognized him from his photo, but was shocked by his age. He couldn't have been older than thirty, yet he held an air of authority.

If I'm honest, the first time I saw him was the beginning of the downhill spiral. His tailored suit that accentuated his ice blue eyes and dusty blonde hair instantly attracted me. And he could tell.

At five-foot-ten, I am not a petite female. I've always favored working out to starving myself to stay thin. I'm not the girl that catches guys' eyes. My dark brown hair and cool blue eyes make a unique look, but most guys back off once they get to know me. I am very strong-willed. I know what I want, and I ask for it. My parents taught me that was the way to make people respect me.

Yes, I thought my boss was very attractive, but I never planned on doing anything about it. I continued to do my job and be as professional as I had always been. Over the next month, I noticed him coming into the office more often. Then, he called me into his office. I thought I was in trouble; he had never called me into his office to speak to him before.

His name was Liam White, and he asked me to call him Liam – right before he bent me over his desk and fucked me. Red flag number 1.

I know it was wrong. He didn't make me do it; he didn't have to. I already wanted to. The entire month since he first walked into the office, I had been fantasizing about him doing just that. He was built and tall, and just my type.

The next month went by and neither of us mentioned anything. By this point, he was in the office almost every day.

One night, I went out for my friend's birthday and I saw him at the upscale bar we were going to end our night at. He was sitting in the back corner and his eyes found mine the second I walked in. We left together and returned to his apartment.

Over the next few months, he wooed me. Taking me to fancy restaurants, trips, and spending a lot of time at his apartment. It was always just the two of us. When we went out we always traveled outside the city. Red flag number 2.

At the office, we kept it professional – at least mostly. Occasionally, I snuck into his office for a quickie, but we kept it quiet. Nobody knew about our secret love affair.

Yes, love. I fell fast. I fell hard. He was everything I wasn't supposed to have. I was everything I told myself I would never be. This was not who I was as a person, but I was determined to be different than the other girls who slept with their bosses.

I had been working for Amtika for two and a half years when I got promoted to research assistant. Or moved to, after I got caught in a compromising position with my boss in his office. I was so excited to finally be working in a lab that I didn't even think about what it would entail.

Hours upon hours of pipetting materials and cleaning glassware and equipment. I buckled down and suffered through it, knowing I needed to pay my dues before I could rise in the ranks.

Even in my new position, I kept seeing glimpses of Liam around the office. It had been two years since we started, in my mind, dating, but I learned he had a different idea of what we were doing. Just as I thought we were heading towards the next step, he completely cut things off. I figured it was because of us getting caught. He wouldn't return any of my messages. In my head I knew it was over, but my heart wasn't ready.

Four months after I switched positions, I confronted him. I needed a final answer as to where we stood.

That was the day I realized that I had never been more than a convenient fuck.

I was determined to not let it affect me. We were just fuck buddies, so why did I care?

But it did affect me. A lot. I thought I was in love with him. He asked me to meet him for dinner to further discuss, but I said no. I couldn't keep torturing myself.

Three years after I started my perfect job, I was miserable. I was doing a job I thought I would love, but actually hated. Every time I stepped into the building I thought of Liam.

Home held a mixture of feelings for me: my lost brother, friends I had alienated, and an underlying feeling I could never seem to brush aside. It was time to return.

My car slows as I crest the last hill on the windy road leading to my town. The snowcapped mountains frame the town, descending into mountainsides of lush, evergreen trees. Something gleaming on one of the hills, towering over the buildings below, catches my eye—The Academy.

As my car crawls along, I know I am trying to push off my arrival home, if even by a few minutes. I'm home, but with that comes painful memories.

Two rights and a left and I find myself pulling up in front of my parents' house. A few flowers peek out of a pot on the wood porch wrapping around the front of the house. Everything looks the same, but I feel like something is different. Something in the air is putting me on edge.

I brush it off as nervousness since I have avoided home for the last seven years.

As I walk into my childhood house, I let out the breath I feel like I've been holding for months. The smell of fresh baked chocolate chip cookies drifts from the kitchen, engulfing me in comfort.

Before I can set my bags down, I'm charged by my dog, Moon, who stayed with my parents when I left for college. Through the excited barks and sloppy kisses, I pet her white, furry head. I remember begging my parents to let me get her as my senior year of high school was winding down. I needed her. I knew I would be leaving for college at UC Denver in only a few, short months. A part of me thought my parents could use a dog. With everything that had happened with my brother, a quiet house would have been too much to handle. My plan was to bring her to live with me once I moved out of the college dorms, but by then, she had adjusted to the mountain lifestyle and it would have been unfair of me to make her live in my small apartment. And, I liked the idea of my parents having a dog around.

My parents live on fifty acres on the outskirts of town. Moon, a beautiful white husky with blue eyes, had grown accustomed to roaming the forests at her will and would have hated living in the city. My parents don't admit it, but Moon turned into their child when I left, even if she is still *my* dog when she does something bad. I've missed her a lot and am glad I'll be spending some much-needed time with her.

Moon's happy yips are so loud, I know they'll alert my parents to my arrival.

They know nothing about Liam and me. I never really told anyone, which should have been an obvious red flag. The past can be so clear, yet we have no option to change it, so it's better not to live there. My parents think I need a change of pace, which is true. I just didn't tell them all the details.

Sure enough, my mother rounds the corner and brightens when she sees me. Wearing black jeans and a blue flannel, she looks exactly the same as the last time I saw her. Except for her eyes, they looked worried and concerned. When she pulls me into a tight hug, I feel more of the tension leave my body. It feels good to be home.

Letting go, I look around and ask, "Where's dad?"

My mom motions for me to come back into the kitchen with her. "He got called into work about an hour ago. Apparently, there was an issue with an elk and a tourist. I swear those tourists must be blind to all the signs and warnings. What's so hard about the concept that you should keep your distance from a wild animal?"

My father is a park ranger at Rocky Mountain National Park. He deals with everything from keeping track of the number of the animals in and around the park, to the onslaught of ignorant tourists that travel here each year. I know the town's main industry is tourism, but sometimes I wish we could just keep this little slice of heaven to ourselves.

Accalia is a medium-sized town that has everything a person could need, from a grocery store, to clothing shops, schools, and even a full hospital, but only about a quarter of its residents live here year-round. During the summer months, the town is flooded with seasonal visitors and tourists that don't want to brave the snow of the Colorado mountains in the winter.

I sit at the table in the kitchen as I watch my mom give Moon a beef stick from the treat jar. That dog is so beyond spoiled, but I am glad they have her. Having a dog seemed to lessen the blow when I left for college.

My mom places a plate of cookies and a glass of milk in front of me. I smile, because it doesn't matter how old I am, I'm always my mom's little girl.

Taking the seat next to me, she asks a question I know has been gnawing at her since I mentioned I would be moving home a few weeks ago. "Jamie, is everything all right?"

It's really not, but I'm not ready to get into the details yet. Some things are better left unsaid, especially the fact that I was sleeping with my boss for over two years. But I know I am not going to get away with saying nothing, so I decide to give the PG version.

"I just felt like I needed a break to think some things through. I worked so hard to get the job I have always dreamed about, and then I hated it. At least when I was working as an assistant, I had a window, and I got to run out and do errands. I couldn't stand being cooped in the labs all day every day."

As I spell it all out for my mom, I cringe at how miserable I was. I tried so hard to make it work, but it wasn't just Liam. I really hated the work.

My mom places her hand on mine. "Sweetheart, it sounds like you made the right decision to close that chapter of your life. Don't try to rush back into things. Stay here as long as you need until you figure out your next direction."

I had been feeling as if I'd let my parents down, but now I know that my mom just wants me to be happy, wherever that may take me. They have been nothing but supportive in all my endeavors. I put a lot of pressure on myself to be perfect because they've already gone through so much with my brother. I don't want them to have any worries with me.

My brother, Jacob, was eight years older than me. When he was eighteen and graduated from high school, he and his friends went camping in the park to celebrate. They were attacked by wild animals and there were no survivors. Such attacks are rare, but they do occur in areas with a lot of wildlife. To this day, it's the only bad thing I can ever remember happening in our small town.

I was young when it happened, and my parents tried to protect me from the details, but as any young child would do, I used the internet to fill in as many gaps as possible. There were few pictures as most were too gruesome to be published, but there was one of a bloody paw print on the tent that still haunts me to this day.

My parents were devastated. Who wouldn't be after losing

a child? Because of the age gap, my brother and I weren't very close, but I still felt a part of me died with him. No matter the situation, losing a sibling is never easy. I never got a chance to really know my brother.

For years we all struggled, my mom most of all. Nobody could figure out what exactly happened and many people in town seemed to have forgotten it even occurred after a few months. My brother was here one day and mysteriously killed the next. It's always felt like unfinished business, but nobody likes to mention it.

As I take a bite of the still-warm cookies, I try not to think about the incident. I came here to relax and become grounded, not to dig up old memories from my past.

I look at my mom when I say, "I think a few weeks of fresh air will do me a lot of good."

She smiles at me as I eat my cookie in silence, thinking about how much has changed since I left my hometown seven years ago.

After moving my stuff out of my car and into the house, I decide to go into town. While the town looks familiar, there are multiple new businesses. I haven't spent much time here since high school. It feels surreal to be back. Since I've been gone, I've been feeling a pull toward the mountains, but for the first time in years, that feeling has disappeared.

It's the middle of June so the town is bustling with tourists enjoying the warm 75-degree temperatures. As I drive down Main Street, I pass families window shopping along the sidewalk as their kids enjoy a variety of sweets from the various candy and ice cream shops on the street.

As I approach the end of Main Street, I pull into a dirt parking lot. The lot is shaded by trees and is situated right next to a creek. Instead of heading toward the street, I follow the short dirt trail along the creek to my favorite coffee shop.

The store is a converted old house, hidden in the trees. It doesn't have a name, it just *is*. Run by an older widow, the coffee shop, combined with books and trinkets, had always been a favorite spot of mine since I was a young girl. Not only is it a great place to get lost in a book, something about the store feels magical. I haven't been here in years, not since I left for college.

As I open the front door the smell of espresso and old books greets me. I smile as the familiarity of the shop eases more of my tension. I walk across the living room area which has been turned into a library, with bookshelves lining the walls and a giant sofa in front of the fire. The couch is currently occupied by a young couple, drinking iced lattes and chatting.

I head towards the kitchen area, which is where they brew the coffee, and see Roberta manning the coffee machine. She has run the bookshop and coffee shop independently for as long as I can remember. She must be getting close to eighty, but she still looks as enthusiastic as ever.

She hands a man I don't recognize a coffee as I step into line behind him. As he turns around to leave, his eyes find my face and linger. He is attractive and I find my body reacting to him instantly. After a few seconds, I start to feel uncomfortable. What does he want?

When he doesn't stop staring, I ask, "What's your problem?" He may be attractive but he is acting like a creep. Plus, I don't like the way my body feels. He is a stranger; it is putting me on edge.

This seems to knock him back into reality. He shakes his head slightly and, without saying anything, leaves.

That was weird. I didn't get a good look at him, other than his eyes, which were a super light brown, almost yellowish color. I've never seen anyone with eyes like that before.

Roberta's voice brings me back. "Oh, if it isn't my little Jamie, all grown up. Come give me a hug!"

She rounds the counter and pulls me into a firm hug. She may have aged a few years, but her spunk hasn't gone anywhere.

Keeping her hands on my shoulders, she moves me back so she can get a better look at me. "Well, haven't you just turned into such a beautiful woman? To what do I owe the pleasure for having you back in my store after so many years? We knew you would be coming back soon."

I used to come here almost every day when I was in high school. Roberta had become like a grandmother to me; being here made me feel safe. I feel guilty for not stopping in before now.

"The store looks great. I'm sorry I never stopped by. I was busy," I attempt vaguely.

"I've heard. The word was you got a bigshot job in the city. We all knew you were going places."

I nod, cringing inwardly. Swiftly switching the subject, I ask, "So what have I missed around here?"

Her expression darkens. "Oh honey, you have been gone a long time. A lot is the same, but there has also been a lot of change. Let me fix you a cappuccino and we can go find a quiet corner to talk."

Drink in hand, I listen as Roberta summarizes the town drama over the last seven years.

"Everyone kept questioning why you left so abruptly for years." I shrink as I think back to those last few weeks before I left. I felt chained. Caged. Part of me kept yelling to run and I listened.

Roberta continues, "The Academy has been taking in more students each year. They asked me to come back and help out."

Sipping my coffee, I'm grateful for the caffeine hitting my bloodstream. "I didn't know you used to work there." I had always had a fascination with the private school that sat on the top of the mountain towering over the town. All my questions seemed to be met with curious looks, as if nobody else noticed the same mysterious private school the town housed.

Roberta gives me a sad smile. "Oh honey, there are a lot

of things you don't know."

Why is she being so cryptic with me? Am I an outsider now that I have been gone for so many years?

Brushing past her words like she didn't mention them. "A few of the tourists have been saying that they have seen wolves around. That has been the hot topic recently. Most people think they are just mistaking dogs or coyotes. Three summers ago, we had a big shot bull rider from Texas try to ride a moose, it obviously didn't end well. He is lucky to be alive"

It feels good to be home, where gossip revolves around animals more than people.

After an hour chatting with Roberta, I decide to walk around Main Street to see which shops are still here and venture into the new ones. As I begin to walk, a moment of déjà vu hits me in a comforting way. My world may have changed a lot recently, but my town is still the same as I remember. It was the right decision to come home.

I've only been here a day, but in my heart, I know I'll never want to leave the mountains again. I feel a connection to this town; I need to stay here.

I stop into one of my favorite stores, a rock shop. The store is filled with geodes and fossils of all shapes and sizes. I'd always found the store fascinating as a kid, seeing the incredible things that had survived after so many years.

As I'm leaving, a necklace catches my eye. I'm not typically a person who likes to wear a lot of jewelry, but something about the soft pink oval jewel on a silver chain calls to me.

After asking the person behind the counter if I could see it, there's no going back. The saleswoman tells me about the hecatolite stone, also known as a moonstone, as I place it around my neck and I know I must get it. As the cashier rings up the price, I cringe a little. Since I'm not currently working, I need to watch how much money I'm spending, but I have to have it. Besides, I can always get a part-time job in town to make a little extra money and fill my time.

Next, I stop at the ice cream shop I remember from my childhood. With my double scoop waffle cone in hand, I step out of the shop, shading my eyes from the sun.

"Jamie? Is that you?"

My eyes are still adjusting to the brightness outside, so it takes me a moment to identify where the voice is coming from.

A man about my age, wearing a police uniform, is walking towards me. As he gets closer, I recognize him and feel stupid for not realizing who it was sooner.

"My, my, Mr. Cleveland, you have grown up mighty fine."

A large smile crosses his face. "Jamie! At first, I thought my eyes were playing tricks on me. What are you doing here?"

People are questioning why I'm here? In my hometown? Now I really know I have been gone too long.

"The mountains were calling, and I needed to come back, at least for a little while." I take a bite of my melting ice cream, feeling a little ridiculous.

He grins at me. "I've got a moment. Why don't we sit down a minute and catch up?"

Before I can think about it, I agree and follow him to a table in front of the ice cream shop.

This is the first time in seven years I have talked to Mark Cleveland. The last time I saw him, I broke off our five-year relationship, right before leaving town. I knew I would most likely see him again, but I didn't think it would happen this quickly.

Chapter 3:

I went on my first date with Mark when I was thirteen. It was the end of eighth grade, and I was still in my gangly, awkward phase. I had braces and I'd grown five inches that year, making me extremely uncoordinated. I was just starting to enter the world of boys.

Many of my friends had already had relationships, most of which did not last longer than a week and maybe included one awkward make-out session.

Mark lived in my neighborhood and had always been one of my friends, even though he was two years older. On the last day of middle school, our friendship started heading in a new direction. He asked me to go to the movies with him. Just him.

Our small town had a one-screen movie theater that shows a movie on Friday and Saturday nights. I don't remember what the movie was. All I remember was that I was nervous. We'd gone to the movies a hundred times together in a group, but this time was different, we were alone.

When he walked me home that night, he kissed me. My teeth bumped against his, it was awkward and awesome at the same time. It was my first kiss and I thought about it all night. Unfortunately, he was leaving for a month-long summer camp the next day where he wouldn't have phone service.

A week after he left, I got my braces off and it was like flipping a switch on my confidence. I'd always been quiet and shy, but with my braces off, and the new hair cut I begged my mom to get, I felt more mature.

When Mark returned, our friendship changed to boyfriend and girlfriend. Over that summer, we became a unit. Jamie and Mark. Everyone knew we were together, and it just worked.

He was a great guy, always the gentleman, but I still wished I had my brother around to put the fear of god in him if he ever did anything wrong.

Mark was one of those guys that had all-American good looks – tall and built, with his light blonde hair and dark blue eyes – and together we made an attractive couple.

I was a young girl in love. At fifteen, I lost my virginity to him. I thought I'd found the man I was going to marry, and we were going to be together forever. We dated all through high school. He left for college in Boulder, but he came home for the weekends, or I went down to visit him at his dorm. It was perfect and we were happy.

Towards the end of my senior year, though, I suddenly began to feel trapped. I loved my town and where I grew up, but I felt stuck. Mark was always planning on coming back and working for the town police. He hoped to become the sheriff one day.

I was going to be a nurse and work at the hospital. It was all planned out and set, and yet something was missing. At eighteen, I felt locked in a cage I would never be able to escape.

I realized I had the overwhelming desire to get out and experience more than just my small town. The feeling was escalated a month before the end of my senior year of high school. I attended a party that would haunt me for the rest of my life.

I chose to start my college classes early and left the day after I graduated high school. Mark was one of the things that was holding me here, so the day before I left, I severed the tie. He was shocked, along with my parents and practically the whole town. We had been a thing for so long, nobody knew how to handle the fact that we weren't together.

That was seven years ago. He'd tried to contact me a few times over the first year, but I was so involved in my new life that I ignored him, all my friends, and everything to do with my old town.

Now I am sitting across from him and with melted ice cream dripping down my hand.

I see a smile on his face, but hurt in his eyes. What do I

do now? I feel melted ice cream start to drip down my hand so I lick it away, grateful for the distraction.

Mark breaks the awkward silence. "How are you Jamie? Are you just in town for the weekend?"

Glad that he is sticking to small talk, I respond, "I'm doing okay. What about you, Mark? I see that you are now part of the town police department, like you always wanted." I intentionally ignore his question, mostly because I don't want him to get any ideas.

He leans back, totally relaxed. I, on the other hand, feel like a bundle of nerves. "Yeah, after college, I went to the police academy, then moved back up here about four years ago to join the department."

More awkward silence. I stand up and say, "My mom is probably waiting on me for dinner, so I should get going. It was good to see you, Mark." Was it good to see him? It just slipped out because I didn't know what else to say.

Mark stands as well, looking at me as if he wants to hug me. I hold up my dripping ice cream cone to deter him.

"It was really good to see you, Jamie. Oh, hey …" He fumbles in his shirt pocket and pulls out a business card. "Here's my card. If you have time, we should meet and catch up."

I smile and walk away, but I feel his eyes on my back the whole time. Fuck. Is he still in love with me?

I throw my now-melted ice cream in the trash and head back to where I parked my car. Great. I've been back in town for less than twenty-four hours and I'm already getting wrapped up in my old life.

After my run-in with Mark, I decide to keep my distance from town for the next few days. I spend it catching up with my parents and hiking around my house with Moon since the forest seems to be calling me. I know I can't ignore Mark forever, but a few more days won't hurt.

On the fourth day, I decide I need to stop being a chicken, so I take my mom up on her offer to go with her to the store. She wants to make steaks for dinner and needs to pick up a few things.

Since my return, she seems flustered and I want to spend time with her to see if I can figure out why. When I asked if she was okay, she brushed me off and ignored the question.

As we drive into town, she points out all the new businesses that have popped up over the years. While Accalia is still small, it has grown a lot in the years I've been gone. My mom points out a new medical building where she works as a part-time nurse.

My mother explains that a new chain grocery store was built on the other side of town a few years ago, but she prefers to support the family-owned store that has been here for as long as I can remember. Inside the store, there is a small grill selling burgers, fries, and other greasy food items. They also have one of the only soft-serve ice cream machines in the town. I have fond memories of eating ice cream as I walked around the store with my mom, and they all come flooding back as we go inside.

We don't make it past the door before someone comes up to talk to us. One thing about the city is that a trip to the store can be quick, since everyone just wants to mind their own business. Not so, here.

By this point, I have my response down for how I am doing and my reason for being home. It's a small town and people are going to speculate so I must give them something. I've been telling them that I missed the mountains and needed a break from the craziness of the city. A few people mention the potential wolf sightings, but nothing else seems to have changed.

I still don't know how long I am planning on staying here, but now that I am back, surrounded by the mountains, I feel more grounded than I have in the last seven years. I had my reasons for running, but now that I am back, I don't want to leave.

I feel like I can't leave.

Chapter 4:

My feet pound on the ground as air rushes over my face. I feel free. Alive. No direction, no destination. I continue to run forward. Pushing my muscles, I power ahead.

Something is chasing me. My hackles rise. Fight or flight. Before I have time to think, claws dig into my back. I'm caught. Danger.

Where is he? He is always around when I need him.

A howl pierces the air, followed by a black streak, flying through the air towards my attacker.

How did I get here? What has my life become?

I shoot up in bed as the dream begins to fade. Drenched in sweat, I feel as if there are claw marks on my back. I ease out of bed for the shower. As I walk into the bathroom, I pull up my shirt to examine my still burning back.

Four red lines mar my skin. What the hell? I watch as

they fade quickly, then begin questioning their very existence. Maybe I haven't fully woken up yet.

As I step into the shower, a lingering concern stays with me – fear.

I love my parents' property, but after walking the trail that circles it for the fifth day in a row, I'm bored. It is time I had a change of scenery. My dream from this morning pops into my head, but I squash the fear. Bad things don't happen in this town.

I think about my brother's mysterious death. We never found out what was responsible, but nothing has happened since.

I know by hiding away at my parents' house, I am just putting off the inevitable. I came home to feel free, not suffocated. Let people talk; it isn't going to change who I am or what I do. I am over others deciding my future. It is mine and I took control of it seven years ago when I left, and I still have control of it now.

I grab my keys off the counter and call for Moon. First, I'll grab coffee and say hi to Roberta, and then we'll go on one of my favorite hikes to Sky Pond.

I'm feeling better already as I get behind the wheel of my car. Fuck everyone else, this is my life and I am not going to live it in fear of what might happen or what people think should've happened.

As I round a bend, something moves in the corner of my eye and runs into the forest. Moon growls from the back seat. I stop the car and peer between the trees, but there's nothing. I could swear it was a wolf. We don't have wolves in Colorado, or at least we didn't when I lived here. The rumors I have been hearing about wolf sightings don't seem so ridiculous now. My dad has a theory that they might be migrating down from Yellowstone, but nobody has been able to confirm it.

Probably just a large coyote. I'll tell my dad about it later.

As I enter town, the building that sits up on the top of the hill next to the park gleams in the early morning light. The Academy, the elite private school that has been there since before I was born. None of the locals attend or can afford to. I know; I wanted to go so badly when I was growing up.

I'd always seen it up there and heard whisperings about it. When Academy kids came into town, they had a superior air to them. The school is small, with no more than ten people per class, and houses all of the students onsite. Primarily a high school, they were known to have a few younger kids if they met their standards.

Not that anyone knew what those standards were. I was a good student in high school and, curious to see what was involved in applying, I tried to research the criteria to attend. Nothing.

They didn't even have a website. According to the internet they didn't exist. I couldn't find any way to contact them. I asked around to see if anyone knew anything about them.

All I got was that they were very exclusive and had many high-profile students. There was a rumor that the President's daughter was enrolled.

After a few weeks of researching and getting nowhere, my parents called me into the living room. They both looked upset. The last time they had done this was when my brother died. I could already feel the tears pricking my eyes as they started to talk.

"Jamie, you know that you are the most important thing in the world to both of us, and we would give you the world, if we could."

All I could think was, *Am I in trouble?* I had never had my parents talk to me like this before.

"We know you have been asking around about The Academy. Yesterday, your dad went to see if it was a possibility. I'm sorry, sweetheart, but there is no way we will be able to afford the tuition. They don't offer scholarships, and the base tuition is $250,000 per year. I really am sorry." The look in her eyes didn't quite match her words, but I couldn't place it.

I knew going to The Academy was a long shot, but that sealed the deal. I shut my mind to the possibility. Something still didn't sit well with me. There were too many unanswered questions.

As I pull up to the coffee shop, a blonde woman is walking down the path toward me. She's holding the hand of a young girl who can't be more than two. Before I see her face, I know it's Tollen, my best friend growing up. I'd know that walk anywhere.

I haven't talked to Tollen in seven years. We used to know everything about each other, but now we are strangers.

I debate if I should just drive away, but at that moment, she looks straight into my eyes. I'm caught. Stepping out of my car, I take a deep breath in preparation.

As I walk towards her, she sends me a smile that's undoubtedly forced. She hasn't changed much since high school. She was always the short, curvy, petite girl all the boys went crazy over. With her round face and chocolate eyes she's still as stunning as she was all those years ago.

Even though I hadn't seen her in seven years, when everything went down with Liam, she is who I wanted to talk to. But I couldn't just reach out to her out of the blue, especially after sealing her out of my life so long ago.

She pulls me into an awkward hug and says, "I heard that you were back in town." The way she says it shows me just how much I hurt her. She's mad and she is not trying to hide it. I would be mad at me, too.

"Hey Tollen. You're looking good. And who might this be?" I squat down so that I'm her daughter's height, but she shies away behind her mom's legs.

In a clipped voice she says, "This is my daughter, Toby."

If there is any hope for us to rekindle our friendship, I know it is going to have to come from me.

"Are you free any night this week? I'd love to take you to dinner and catch up."

I can tell the instincts within her are warring with one another by the way she hesitates, but she says, "I'll see if I can make it work. Do you still have the same number?"

I nod. If she had any suspicion that I ignored her all these years, this confirms it. My number never changed; I got every one of her messages.

She walks to her car and gets her daughter situated into her car seat. She doesn't say another word as she climbs behind the driver's seat and pulls out.

Now needing coffee desperately, I grab Moon's leash and we walk up the trail to the coffee shop. I hope once I explain myself, all my friends will stop hating me. If they don't, I'll deserve it.

Chapter 5:

With my headphones in and my feet pounding against the ground, I set a blistering pace up the trail. I've covered three miles and I've only been hiking for forty minutes. Moon is trotting happily in front of me, occasionally chasing a squirrel or stopping to smell since I took her off the leash after we couldn't see the road any longer.

Mountains rise sharply on both sides of me, but I am too caught up in my head to be able to enjoy the beauty.

Yes, my job was bad, but I could have just applied for a new one. Yes, there was the whole Liam thing, but I could have found a new guy. Why was my instinct to run? And why was home where I wanted to come back to when I had felt so trapped here before I left? Why do I feel like I *need* to be here, in Accalia, when it was the last place I'd wanted to be the last seven years?

I'm so lost in thought that I trip and face-plant in the dirt. Shit. My hands sting from sliding in the dirt and my knee throbs from impact with a rock. Embarrassed and wallowing in self-pity, I stay in the dirt for a moment, until Moon comes up and licks my face, asking if I am all right.

I'm not, but it has nothing to do with falling on my face and everything to do with the shitshow that is my life. I have nobody to blame but myself.

Since I still have my headphones in, I don't hear someone walking up behind me. I jump when a hand lands firmly on my shoulder, flipping over and sitting up as one of my earbuds falls out.

The man in front of me has light brown, almost yellow eyes, and is squatting so that he's at my height with a concerned look on his face. It's the man from the coffee shop. He'd been staring at me before, but now, *I'm* the one who is so lost staring into his eyes. I don't hear his words.

A second, or maybe a lifetime, passes before he waves his hand in front of my face. "Are you all right?"

No, the current state of my life is a shitshow, but he isn't asking me about that. I'm lying in the dirt, in the middle of the path, bruised and scraped.

I nod and start to stand up. He offers his hand, so I take it. As our hands connect, I feel a jolt, as if electricity was flowing from one of us to the other. His hand is warm, and he pulls me to my feet with ease.

As he does, I get a better look at him. He has slightly messy brown hair and a serious look on his face that doesn't reach his eyes, which are warm and welcoming. And I have to look *way* up to see his face, because he's at least a few inches above six feet. His frame is muscular and built without being bulky. I have time to get a full look, not just the quick peek I had at the coffee shop.

And he's extremely attractive. I'm at a loss for words.

I hear Moon growl from next to me as she moves between this mystery guy and me. He looks down at her and she instantly stops. Weird.

He reaches out to brush some hair away from my face. "Did you hit your head?"

I lean into his touch, wanting to feel that jolt again. *Jamie get your act together. What's wrong with you?*

I take a step back and a small flicker of hurt crosses his face. Why? I just met him, after all. Maybe it's because something about him seems so familiar.

Finding my voice, I say, "Yeah I am fine, thanks for the help. I guess I got a little distracted and didn't see that rock. It's mostly just my ego that's bruised." I laugh at myself but the guy doesn't join.

"You're lucky you didn't slam your head into a rock," he says, oddly concerned over someone he's just met. I can't seem to get a read on this guy.

"Well, thanks for your concern. I'm Jamie."

"Wren. You need to be more careful." He sounds almost pissed, as if I bruised *him* instead of myself.

This guy may be attractive, and he helped me out, but what gives him the right to treat me like a misbehaving child?

"Well Wren, thank you for the assistance, but I've got it from here. I hope you enjoy the rest of your walk." Brushing my dirty hands on my thighs, I continue down the trail.

It takes all my willpower not to turn around and look back at Wren. Such an unusual name for an unusual man.

For the rest of the walk, my mind is clouded with thoughts of him. There is something about him that I just can't put my finger on.

Chapter 6:

As I walk in the front door of my parents' house, I'm hit with the aroma of food coming from the kitchen. It's so much better than walking into a dark, empty apartment. Even when I was with Liam, he never stayed at my apartment and rarely asked me to stay the night at his. Yet another sign I should've recognized.

Shaking away those thoughts, I stop in my tracks when I walk into the kitchen.

Wren is sitting at the kitchen island, smiling at me. My stomach flips as his eyes connect with mine.

What is he doing here?

My mom can see I'm confused. "Jamie, you know Wren, don't you? He went to The Academy when you were in high school. I believe you guys are around the same age. He just moved back to town and is starting up as a ranger with the park."

Maybe that's why he seems so familiar. There is something about his eyes that I just don't think I could forget. He stands and offers his hand with the same seriousness as when he was helping me in the forest. Something about his look makes me feel as if he is a predator assessing his prey.

"Jamie, it's nice to officially meet you again. Your dad talks about you a lot. He is very proud of you." Nervousness bubbles inside me the longer I am near him.

I'm surprised by his words. I never get that feeling from my dad. He always seems to be pushing me towards doing more, making me think what I am isn't enough. He has always wanted me to leave this small town and build a successful life elsewhere. When I left abruptly, he was the only one who seemed happy for me.

Something about this guy puts me on edge, but I take his hand anyway, feeling the sharp jolt of electricity, again. I try to pull my hand away, but he tightens his grip, making me hold his for a few more seconds. The look he is giving me is filled with familiarity. Possessiveness.

I realize what is putting me on edge with Wren. I feel drawn to him. An attraction, but on a more primal level, stronger than I've ever felt before.

My mind screams that he's dangerous, that I need to get away. *What is going on?*

Moon scampers into the kitchen following the smell of food. When she sees Wren, she lets out a small growl. I place my hand on her head but don't tell her to stop. Moon obviously feels some of the tension I feel.

My dad walks in the door, a large smile appearing on his face when he sees Wren. He's obviously fond of him by the way he claps him on the shoulder. "Wren, if you aren't busy, why don't you join us for dinner?" Sometimes I wish my dad wasn't such a nice guy.

"I'd really like that, Mr. Carter."

"Wren, call me John when we aren't at work. Want to grab a beer and I'll give you a tour of the house?" His voice trailing off as they walk out of the kitchen.

Once they are out of hearing distance I turn to my mom. "What is he doing here?" My tone is harsher than I intended, and my mom catches onto it.

She reaches over the table and pushes something towards me. I look down to see my necklace with the pink jewel. My hand immediately goes to my neck. It's gone.

Ignoring my hostility, she replies, "He's returning your necklace. He said you dropped it on your hike today. That doesn't look cheap. I would be grateful he returned it."

How did Wren know where I lived?

I take the necklace and fasten it around my neck. I mumble something about needing a shower and then head up to my room.

As I'm walking up the stairs, I run into Wren and my father. Wren's eyes track to the necklace around my neck.

"I'm glad I was able to return that to you. It looks very good on you."

"Thank you. I hadn't even realized I was missing it." I am

grateful. I know I just bought this necklace less than a week ago, but it feels like part of me already. Wren still puts me on edge, though. Maybe if I could think of where I've seen him before, it wouldn't bother me so much.

My dad says something about showing him his new sailboat before dinner.

As they walk past me, I feel Wren's arm brush against mine leaving a tingling sensation.

Marking it up to static electricity, I head up to the bathroom.

As the water flows over me, I try to rack my brain for why Wren looks so familiar. I went to one Academy party, my senior year. Maybe he was there? It's the eyes. I know those eyes.

I know dinner's soon, so not wanting to keep them waiting, I dry my hair quickly and throw on a summer dress.

I pause as I'm walking out the door and decide to put on a little mascara. I tell myself I am doing it for myself, but I know it's because Wren is here. Whoever he may be.

I am walking up the path to the coffee shop the next morning when my mind drifts back to dinner. Wren seems like a nice man who obviously came from money, since he attended The Academy. All during our meal, I kept trying to find something to dislike about him. I don't know why. Something about him makes my skin prickle, but I can't put my finger on it.

My parents seem to love him. My father is impressed with him. He's only been working with the rangers for a few months, but he has already become a valuable asset to the team, according to my father.

Who the fuck does this Wren guy think he is and why do I care? He was nothing but polite. He didn't try to make any moves and he returned my necklace. Ugh, I need coffee.

My hand drifts up to my necklace and I finger the smooth pink stone. How did it manage to fall off in the woods? The clasp was undamaged. Maybe I did hit my head and just couldn't remember.

Lost in thought, I bump straight into a large male's chest as I open the door to the coffee shop. Before I look up, I already know who it is. I dated Mark for five years, after all.

He's dressed in normal clothes today, holding a coffee in one hand and a book in the other. I babble awkwardly to fill the silence.

"Hey Mark, I'm sorry about that."

"Still living with your head in the clouds, huh, Jamie?" He grins, but then turns serious. "I wanted to run into you, though. We need to talk."

I groan inwardly. "About what?"

"I'm not sure how long you will be staying in town, but we're bound to run into each other from time to time. We were friends before we ever started dating and I would hate to lose that forever."

When he puts it that way, he makes me feel like the big

bad witch who took advantage of a poor, innocent boy. Hell, I have nothing else to do and he is right. We need to talk, if only so I can set him straight about "us".

"Fine. Want to sit at our table and I'll meet you out there once I have my coffee?"

He raises an eyebrow and his face turns confused.

I don't realize what I had said until after I walk inside the shop. *Our table*. Shit, it's so easy to fall into old patterns.

Just so that it doesn't feel like old times, I order something new. Taking a sip of the latte, I know this will be my new drink because every time I drink it, it will remind me of finally taking control of my life.

As I sit across from Mark, he starts talking. "Jamie. God, I've wanted to talk to you for so long. When you left, I was mad. I loved you and I know you loved me back. One day we were discussing the rest of our lives, and the next you were just gone. You never returned any of my phone calls or texts. Then I started hating you. I hated you so much, I thought if I ever saw you again, I might not even be able to speak to you."

I try to speak, but he holds up a hand.

"I need to get this out. Please let me just finish before you say anything. I was confused. We were still young, and I felt lost without you. You were part of my life, not just as a lover but as a friend. You were my best friend, and I couldn't even talk to you when I needed you. About three and a half years after you left, my dad died in a car accident. I had just moved home a week before and I was starting my job with the

Accalia police department the next day.

"From his tire track they could tell he swerved to try to miss something running across the road and lost control of the car. And in a second, everything in my parents' life was different. This put everything in perspective. I didn't know what you were going through or why you left, but I knew I wasn't going to be part of your life any longer and I needed to get over it.

"I built a new life and tried to just remember the good memories. We really did have a good thing going, Jamie. I could have made you happy if you would have just talked to me."

Why did I never talk to him? I know he would have understood; he always understood. He knew me better than anyone. I take a moment to gather my thoughts. My mom had mentioned his father died, and I'd thought about calling him. In the end, I hadn't. It had been a long time, and I figured I was the last person he wanted to talk to.

"Mark, first I want to apologize. I *need* to give you an apology. I know it won't do much now. What I did should make you hate me for the rest of your life. I could have handled it better. My only excuse is that I was young and panicked. I was starting to feel like I needed to get away, but there was one thing that really put me over the edge.

"I also need to apologize for not telling you what I am about to tell you." I close my eyes and take a deep breath. I have never told anybody this, not even my mother or Tollen.

I'm only telling Mark now because maybe it will help him gain closure on why I left. Or selfishly because I need to get it off my chest. It has been nagging me more since I came home.

"It was late March of my senior year; you had exams coming up, so we decided to not meet up. I was in town on a Saturday with Tollen when a few of The Academy boys asked us if we wanted to go to a party. I wasn't sure. We had never been invited before and I had a bad feeling, but Tollen begged me until I agreed to go with her.

"They gave us the address and we showed up at eight, when they said it started. The house was up on the hill, it was huge, and we were both impressed. We were the only townies there and I felt awkward. It was obvious one of the boys was attracted to Tollen and I was only invited because they knew she wouldn't come alone.

"I sat with them and accepted a drink. They were nice but we just didn't have enough in common. Tollen had disappeared and I knew she was hooking up with The Academy guy. I needed to pee, so I went looking for the restroom. That is when stuff started to get weird.

"As I was looking for the bathroom, I walked into a bedroom. There was a guy standing by the window just looking out over the town below. Something about him drew me in. I closed the door and just started walking towards him. It didn't feel like I was controlling myself, it was like something else was moving my body.

"I didn't get a good look at the guy's face because before

either of us could say anything, we were kissing." I look up at Mark. There is hurt in his eyes and the guilt inside is as strong now as it was then. "It was like I wasn't consciously making my own decisions. Every cell in my body was screaming that I needed him. Needed to be with him."

I don't want to get into details because I know that'll only hurt Mark more but, somehow, I can't help myself.

"We were like animals tearing at each other's clothes. There was this need in me I had never felt before or since. It was fast and full of desperation. As soon as it was over, he pulled on his pants and left. Just walked out the door. I was so confused and shameful, I never told anyone. I couldn't explain it to myself, let alone anyone else. I dressed quickly then snuck out to the car before anyone could see me. I texted Tollen that I was in the car and wanted to leave. I never went back to another Academy party.

"That month, I was late. I was terrified. I knew you would step up no matter what, but I was being eaten up by guilt. I had already felt trapped, and when I thought I could be pregnant, it pushed me over the edge. That was when I realized I didn't want to be trapped in this small town.

"It turned out to be a false alarm. I didn't talk to anyone, even then, because I didn't want anyone to try and bring me back. I was running away. Now I am running back."

We say nothing for a long time. I know I fucked up.

He stands up and looks at me. There is pain in his eyes. "Jamie, I had hoped that we could at least be friends. You were such a big part of my life and I missed having you to talk to. But I am going to need time to decide if we can be."

On that, he walks off the back patio without looking back.

Chapter 7:

I have really made a mess of my life. Would it have been so bad to marry Mark and live in this beautiful place? I had it all and then I just threw it all down the drain.

That night still haunts me. Why didn't I just walk out? What drove me toward that boy I had never met? Was I so desperate to get out that I had to sabotage myself?

As I have done a hundred times before, I try to pack it away in a little box in hopes I will forget about it.

Maybe I should just go back to the city, or a new city, get a different job, start fresh. Why do I still feel so drawn to this damn town, even after what happened?

I spend such a long time thinking about it that by the time I bring my latte to my lips, it's already cold. The chair next to me scrapes on the ground as it is pulled out. I look over to see Roberta sitting down.

"Are you all right, honey? You've been out here staring at nothing for the last hour."

I'm about to tell her I'm fine and not to worry, but then I think of the look on Mark's face. I can't stand to hold it inside anymore.

I spill it all.

Everything. When I'm done, she stares at me for a long time, not speaking. Then, she slowly rises from the table.

"Well, haven't you gotten yourself into a right pickle. I think this is a conversation that needs refreshments. I will be right back."

A few minutes later, Roberta returns with two iced chais and two chocolate-covered coconut macaroons.

"All right, Jamie, let's start with an easy fix. You said you want to stay in town? How would you like to work for me a few mornings a week?"

Of all the directions I thought the conversation would go in, this was not one I expected. But now that she mentions it, I have been thinking of getting a part time job until I figure out what I want to do. Books and coffee, two of my favorite things.

I raise an eyebrow. "Are you just making this position because you feel bad for me or do you actually need help?"

"You're a smart girl, which is one of the reasons I have always liked you. To answer your question, I've been thinking about hiring someone else to help me through the summer. It would be nice to have a few mornings off a week. Plus, it will help me keep an eye on you."

I've always loved this place and I am not ready to start

looking for a full-time job yet. "Yes Roberta, I'd love to work for you. That way, I can make a little money."

Roberta nods. "All right, now that we have that done, what else? Why did you feel you needed to leave?"

For the next few hours, we go through each problem one by one, and at the end of it, I feel better, clearer. I know talking about it isn't going to fix anything, but at least my thoughts aren't as jumbled as they were.

First things first, I need to repair my friendship with Tollen. She was my best friend and I don't know much about her anymore at all. I don't even know who her husband is.

But by the time we're done, the sun is setting, so I decide to wait until tomorrow. Tomorrow, I will begin to fix everything.

I wake up the next day with a mission. After ignoring Tollen for seven years, I'm going to try and get her to go to dinner with me. I know if I can just talk to her, we can repair our friendship. Hopefully.

My mom told me that Tollen works at one of the art galleries in town. I feel kind of bad ambushing her when she is at work, but she hasn't returned any of my texts or calls. Although, I don't blame her, since I ignored her for seven years.

As I open the door, the bell over the door rings. I know she is alone because I have been waiting outside for an opportunity when there isn't anyone else in the shop.

She calls a cheery, "One second!" from the back as I take a moment to look around. On the wall to my right, there are nature photographs of the beauty that surrounds our town. People take it for granted when they see it every day, but it really is mesmerizing. On the other wall, there are paintings of Colorado's nature and mountains, done in different styles.

I'm studying a watercolor painting of a wolf when I hear feet shuffle behind me. Tollen rounds the corner with a big smile on her face, which instantly dies when she sees me. Again, I don't blame her, but it still hurts.

"What do you want, Jamie?"

Maybe this is a bad idea.

No, I'm here, and it's never going to get any better if we don't talk.

"Tollen, I just want to talk, but you won't respond to any of my texts or calls."

"Feels pretty shitty, doesn't it?"

"Okay, I deserved that. And a lot more. What I did was shitty, and my reason for doing it will probably not be enough, but I'm asking you to give me a chance. Let me take you to dinner and at least tell you my side of the story." For the next moment, a debate takes place behind her eyes. Finally, she sighs.

"Fine. You have one shot, so don't mess it up. Toby's dad doesn't work tonight so I can ask him to watch her. I'll text you my address and you can pick me up at six. And I will be ordering at least three drinks, so no cheaping out on me."

With that, an older couple comes in, and I know our conversation is over. She said yes to dinner at least. It's a start.

Chapter 8:

What do you wear to dinner with the best friend you've ignored for the last seven years?

I really didn't think she would say yes and now I'm panicked about the details. I want to keep it casual, but don't want to look cheap. I decide on the Italian restaurant and call ahead to make a reservation.

Opting for a nice pair of jeans, tank top, and sandals, I head to my car so I can pick up Tollen. As I start to drive, my hand goes to my necklace and I will myself to be strong. This is going to be rough, but I must face my previous actions if I want to stay in town.

Fifteen minutes later, I pull up to a small house situated up on the hill right outside of town. The house is light blue with a white fence surrounding the front garden. As I get out and walk to the front door, I get a better look at her garden. It's beautiful. Flowers of every color pour out of the beds and there is a vine climbing up a trellis with a bench under it.

As I am thinking it would be the perfect place to sit and read a book, the front door opens and Tollen appears. She's traded her work clothes for jeans and a T-shirt. Happy that I went with jeans instead of a dress, I raise my hand to wave.

She doesn't respond, just turns around, locks her door and heads to the passenger side of my car. Neither of us say a word during the short drive or as we're first seated at the table.

After our waiter comes over for our drink order, I finally decide to break the silence.

"Let me just start by saying, I'm sorry. I know it will never be enough, but I really am sorry. I had my reasons for leaving, but I could have at least talked to you."

I'm interrupted as our waiter brings our drinks. As I say thank you and begin to talk again, Tollen cuts me off.

"You know the whole world doesn't revolve around you. We've all been fine without you and we'll be fine again as soon as you run off again." Grabbing her drink, she takes a sip.

Okay, maybe I'm going about this the wrong way.

"Why don't you tell me about Toby? She is adorable."

At the mention of her daughter, she brightens slightly. She smiles. "I was finishing up my degree when I found out I was pregnant with her. Luckily, she waited until after finals to be born. I'd already planned on moving home but when I had Toby, I knew I wanted to be around family. She's the best thing that's ever happened to me. You know, all I ever wanted to do was be a mother. I lived with my parents originally, but as soon as we could afford it, we moved out."

She finishes and I realize she didn't mention anything about a father or a husband. My curiosity is piqued, but this is not the time to dig for information. So, I give her my life update, not really sure she cares, but it's better than sitting in silence.

I finish with, "Pretty much as soon as I arrived back in town, I realized how much I missed it here. So, I've decided to stay."

I can tell my last sentence shocks her. She expected me just to pop back into town for a little while and then leave again. From my track record, it would be an accurate assumption.

We order food and I try to keep the conversation light, but she isn't biting. She is clearly done with me. As dessert arrives, I know I have to do something. Something drastic.

"I know you think I went on to greener pastures, but I didn't. It's been terrible. I've always felt a part of me being pulled back, telling me I shouldn't have left. I was scared that if I kept any contact, I would get sucked back. I missed you, and it broke my heart every time I ignored you, but I felt like I needed to be away. I'm only back now because it felt like it was time. Before I left the city, I had hit rock bottom.

"I slept with my boss. Let me finish before you start judging me. I fell in love with him. I thought I would be spending the rest of my life with him and then he dropped me as if I was nothing. That was when I realized I had embellished our relationship. Or lack of relationship. On top of that, I despised my job. It broke something inside of me to realize what I had always dreamed of doing was not what I thought it would be. As things got worse, I realized I needed to return and be surrounded by the mountains."

Tollen, who's working on the third drink I promised her, just stares at me.

After drinking the rest of her wine in one big pull, she tilts her head at me. "Please tell me he was at least hot and not some fifty-year-old fat guy."

I can't help but laugh. Tollen joins in as the reality of the situation sets in. My life is like a bad soap opera. Seriously, who has this much drama in real life?

"He was very attractive and only in his early thirties. I was stupid and got attached and then he traded me in for the newer model. I feel incredibly stupid."

To my surprise, she takes my hand and looks me in the eyes, "We all make mistakes. We are human, it is what we do. But sometimes those mistakes turn into miracles."

We finish dessert and I drive Tollen home. The atmosphere in the car is less tense than it was on the way to the restaurant and I feel like we're making progress. I don't want to rush it, but I miss my best friend.

As we pull up in front of Tollen's house, I wait for her to jump out, but she just sits there. I can tell she wants to say something. I expected a lot of things to come out of her mouth but not what she says.

It comes out in a rush, like she needs to get the words out

as fast as possible.

"Mark is Toby's father."

What?

Mark? As in my ex-boyfriend, Mark? The one that will probably never talk to me again after what I told him yesterday, Mark?

Before I can find my words, Tollen gets out of the car, says thank you for dinner and heads toward her house.

I have no right to be angry, but I am. Mark was always mine. We were each other's. Even when I left, I still thought of him as my Mark. I know it's not fair, and by no means did I stay away from other guys during the last seven years. But I'd never move in on my best friend's boyfriend? She had to know that I'd be upset if I ever saw her again. Did she do it just to spite me?

I have so many questions flying around in my head. I debate walking up to her door and demanding answers, but I'm too angry to talk to her right now.

Instead I head to Roy's, a local bar, for a drink. Typically, I'm not much of a drinker but at the moment I just need to forget, at least for one night. On top of everything, this is just too much.

Ordering a Sea Breeze, I find a table in the corner and take the time to organize my thoughts. Or forget them. I haven't decided yet.

Time flies by, and I've had five drinks before I realize it. When I was eighteen, I thought life was so difficult and every little thing was such a huge deal. It wasn't, but now my life is a true disaster.

Alienate all my friends and make them hate me, check.

Ruin my career by sleeping with my boss, check.

Best friend and ex-boyfriend hook up which leads to a baby, check.

Shit.

Seriously what else could possibly go wrong?

I need some air.

I stand up to head outside. I'm a little wobbly, but somehow make it to the door. I know I can't drive and there are no Ubers up here. Delaying the inevitable, I lean against my car and look up at the stars while I contemplate who to call.

My parents will lecture me about being irresponsible, Mark hates me, and I still don't think I can control my anger around Tollen.

As if he could read my mind, someone says, "Do you need a ride?"

I lower my eyes and stare directly into those yellow brown eyes I find so fascinating. Wren.

I barely know this guy. Isn't accepting rides from strangers when you're drunk like the number one don't on the list? But I really don't have much of an option unless I want to wake my parents, since it's close to midnight.

"Sure, that would be great." As I push off the car, I'm

even more off-balance than before. I forgot to account for the higher altitude when I was drinking. I'm smashed.

Tripping over my own feet, I wait to feel the gravel against my face but instead feel hands wrapping around my arms. Wren catches me and now I'm pressed up against his hard chest. I feel heat everywhere our bodies touch. The attraction I have been trying to squash between us flares up as I get a closer look at him. He is really tall. The top of my head comes only below his chin.

Before I have time to think, I get up on my tippy toes and pull his lips to mine.

An explosion of sparks ignites as our lips meld together. My body fills with a desire that I have only ever felt once in my life. I need him. Every cell in my body is screaming for me to take him. There is an animal need inside me clawing to get out.

I try to pull him closer, but, at the same time, he holds me out at arm's length. We are both breathing heavy and I can see the same desire mirrored in his eyes.

He feels the pull, too.

"Jamie," he breathes. The way he says my name only makes me want him more. Nobody is around and I'm trying to see where we could go that isn't in the middle of an open parking lot.

As if reading my mind, Wren starts to talk. "We can't do it here. Plus, when I have you again, I want you in my bed and I want you to remember."

Have me again? My brain feels fuzzier and fuzzier and my last thought before I black out is, *Who is Wren?*

Chapter 9:

$\mathcal{I}$ feel like death.

I don't open my eyes as I regain consciousness. Ouch. I knew I would regret drinking so much last night, but at the time it seemed like such an easy solution to all my problems.

Seriously, I don't remember feeling this bad before, even in college. Must be the higher altitude.

After a few more minutes, I attempt to pry my eyes open. I need water and drugs.

It takes me a second to realize I don't recognize my surroundings. Quickly, I check to see if I am dressed and am relieved to find that I am. Where am I?

I look around the large room and take in the dark wood furniture and the dark green bedspread I'm lying on. Everything looks expensive and the room is filled with neutral colors.

Slowly, I ease out of bed and head toward the bathroom I see attached to the bedroom. As I walk in, I'm shocked by its size. It's bigger than my bedroom at my parents' house. I look longingly at the shower but decide to stick with splashing some cold water on my face.

Feeling slightly more human, I go in search of the coffee creating the aroma I smell. As I put my hand on the door handle, it swings open. In front of me, Wren is standing there with two cups of coffee.

The sense of need I feel every time I see him resurges. He hands me the coffee and heads to the other side of the room. Is he as affected as I am? Grateful for the coffee and the distance, I thank him. Why do I feel this way?

I take a moment to take him in as I bring the warm coffee up for a drink. Everything about him screams danger. From his dark jeans to his stoic face, he fits the bad boy look perfectly.

After a few moments of silence, he asks, "How are you feeling? After you passed out, I wanted to make sure you were all right. I brought you back here so I could keep an eye on you."

When I think back on last night, I remember dinner with Tollen, her admission about Mark, drinking too much … and then it gets a little fuzzy.

"About as good as I deserve. I way overdid it last night." He nods in agreement. My eyes don't seem to want to leave Wren's as I watch him casually lean against the wall. His white t-shirt stretches across his chest. The faint outline of a tattoo is visible through his shirt, and I have the urge to run my hands over it.

Suddenly, I remember kissing him. I really did that, didn't I? And he kissed me back. Yes, I am attracted to him, but there is also something that makes me nervous. Until I can figure him out, it's best we don't extend our relationship to the physical.

After a few more beats of silence, Wren says, "Well, if you are going to puke, please do it in the toilet. I'll be downstairs when you are ready. I'll drive you home."

On that, he walks out of the room.

He is so strange.

And for whatever reason, that just adds to the appeal.

After finishing my coffee, I find my way downstairs, looking for Wren to drive me back to my car. As I walk through the hallways in the massive, modern house, I feel like I'm wandering through a labyrinth. I find Wren in the kitchen, finishing his coffee. He motions to the door and I follow him out to his car. His eyes dart around nervously to the forest as we step outside, but I see nothing to be concerned about.

A man of few words, he drops me at my car ten minutes later.

After I get out of his car, he rolls his window down and says the first words he's said to me since he brought me my coffee. "Please be careful. You're lucky it was me you ran into last night and not someone who could have taken advantage of you. I put my number in your phone. If you ever need another ride, call me."

With that, he drives away leaving me to wonder. I pull my phone out of my pocket and check it. Sure enough, his number is there, under W in my contacts. How did he get through my Touch ID? I feel like I have whiplash from the hot and cold coming from Wren.

As I get in my car, I decide that I need more time to recover from my hangover before I head home. Breakfast it is.

Earlier that morning, after seeing multiple missed calls from my parents, I sent them a text saying I'd spent the night at a friend's house. They will probably assume it is Tollen, since growing up, we were constantly sleeping at each other's house. They don't need to know everything.

I pull up at The Sundance, my favorite breakfast place. It's still early so I have the place mostly to myself as I venture over to my favorite table in the corner. The table has a stunning view of the mountains, making it the perfect spot to enjoy breakfast.

Grateful for my second cup of coffee of the day, which the waitress poured the moment I arrived, I look over the menu, perusing the options to see if they've changed since the last time I was here. They haven't.

As I'm debating between pancakes and an omelet, the doorbell jingles and I look up.

Shit.

It's Mark and Toby. Before I can look away, my eyes lock

with Mark's.

No going back now. I wave them over.

Sometime in my drunken haze last night, I decided that if I want Tollen and Mark to forgive me, I will have to forgive them as well. Might as well start now.

Mark looks worried, but he directs Toby towards the table, holding her hand. She gives me a shy look.

Mark places her in a chair as he goes to find a booster seat.

Toby and I stare at each other. I have never been sized up by a three-year-old, but that's how this interaction feels.

Mark comes back with a booster seat chair attachment. Once Toby is situated, he looks at me.

"Rough night?"

I realize I must look like crap. I couldn't find a brush in Wren's bathroom, so my hair is in a messy bun and I'm still wearing yesterday's makeup.

"You might say that."

To my surprise, Mark takes my hand. "Jamie, I'm sorry if I freaked out at you the other day. It was a shock and I have to admit I'm still not over the way we ended things. But I'm still your friend, like I've always been, and if you need someone to talk to, I'm here."

Mark is such a nice guy, I forgot just how much of a big teddy bear he was. Before I can respond, Toby says something about Mickey Mouse Pancakes and whipped cream. Mark asks me what I want and then heads up to the bar to order, again leaving me with Toby. Something about that small gesture makes my heart warm.

For the rest of breakfast, we keep the conversation light as Toby makes a mess of herself, eating her food with her hands.

As we walk out, I feel better. Baby steps.

After Mark has Toby strapped into her car seat, he turns to me. "So, I take it Tollen told you about Toby being my daughter."

I nod.

"I just want to let you know it only happened once. It was a few weeks after my dad died, I was upset, and she comforted me. We both had way too much to drink. I wouldn't take it back. I love Toby, but I just wanted you to know. Tollen feels extra guilty about it; maybe you could talk to her." I see hope in his eyes and wonder if there is something between them or Mark wishes there was.

He has no reason to feel ashamed. He didn't cheat on me; we weren't together and hadn't been for a long time. But a selfish part of me is happy to hear it was only a one-night thing.

I lean in and give Mark a hug. "Next time you have a free day you should let me know. We need to catch up some more. Last time we only really talked about me; I want to hear what you have been up to. My number is the same, is yours?"

He nods, and I feel guilty like I did with Tollen.

I can tell from the look in his face what he's thinking. Yes, I got every text and call, but I never responded.

Chapter 10:

It's my first day working at Roberta's, and I'm exhausted. I haven't stopped moving for the last six hours. As noon rolls around, there's finally a break in the traffic. I collapse on the couch. Roberta showed me the ropes a few days ago and I thought I had it down, but I didn't expect so many people to stop in for their morning coffee.

Granted, starting my first day on a Saturday during tourist season was not my best idea. But I did it!

Just as I am getting comfortable, the bells over the door jingle. Fully stretched out on the couch and ready to die, I look up to see Wren's face hovering above me.

A small flicker of a smile crosses his face before his typical serious look reappears. I start to get up, but he motions me to stay down.

He sits in the overstuffed armchair next to the couch and asks, "Busy morning?"

I let out an exasperated sigh. "I have no idea how Roberta

does this all on her own, it was crazy busy all morning."

"She is something special. Has more spunk and energy than someone a third her age." I would agree with that. I don't know why she hasn't gotten help before now. But I suspect she only offered me the job because she knew I needed something to focus on, not because she needed help.

"You want coffee?"

His reply surprises me. "I actually came to see you."

Why would he come to see me? Yes, he let me sleep at his house the other night, but we are still basically strangers.

I smile. "Well, you see me. What's up?"

"You."

I laugh. I'm about as down as one can get.

"I'm serious. I can't seem to stop thinking about you." He gets up and starts pacing. "You don't seem to remember, but we kissed the other night. I feel connected to you. It's always been there, but it's gotten stronger since you returned."

My tired brain is trying to follow his words. Since I returned? But I had never met him before I came back home. Had I?

Wait. Hadn't he said that before, when I was drinking? What does that mean?

The bell above the door dings, altering me to more customers.

Wren walks over to the counter as I do. He pulls me in roughly and slams his lips against mine, hard, pulling away just as quickly.

He wags a finger at me while I try to stop my knees from wobbling. "We need to talk, in private." Then he walks out the door.

What the fuck?

I do my best to compose myself so I can help the family that just walked into the shop.

Yeah. I'd say we *definitely* need to talk.

Roberta comes in at 2 pm to relieve me and we share a cup of tea while discussing the morning. I tell her I don't know how she still works this hard at her age, since I'm practically dead on my feet. She gives me a knowing smile and tells me to enjoy my afternoon.

As I walk out the door, my phone rings. I answer it without looking since I'm too busy trying to find my keys in my purse.

"Hello?"

The voice that replies is not one I expected, nor is it one I thought I would ever hear again.

"Hi Jamie, I get the feeling you were expecting someone else."

I would recognize his voice anywhere. I was in love with him. How could I forget it?

My voice comes off a little harsher than I planned. "Hello, Liam. What do you want?"

"Can I not check in to see how you are?"

We haven't talked in months, not since he told me that what we had was just a hookup and was over. And he thinks *now* is a great time to check in? Who does he think he is? He made it very clear that he didn't want a relationship.

"No, Liam, you can't."

There is a pause and then his voice comes through the line, quieter than before. "I miss you, Jamie."

God dammit! As if my head wasn't already screwed up enough. I throw on my mental armor and pull out my claws before replying.

"You do not have the right to call me and tell me that, Liam. You made it clear we were nothing more than temporary fuck buddies, and I have moved on. Please don't call me again. I'm sure your new girl can keep you entertained."

On that, I hang up and let out a frustrated scream. Who does he think he is?

Now that I am not easily available, he wants me again. But for how long? I'm sure he can find another way to get laid. Why is he bothering me?

I get in my car and start driving, but I don't head home. Instead, I head towards one of my favorite trails. I need to clear my head.

I pound my feet aggressively against the ground as I wind through the trees along the path. Even being out in nature isn't helping the fury building inside of me.

How dare he?

It's been months since we've talked. I never even told him I was leaving town. I wonder if he just realized I was gone and that is why he called. I've only been home for nine days, even though it feels much longer with everything that has been going on.

My phone dings and I see a text from Wren. *Hey,* is all it says. When did he get my number? Probably when he was busy entering his into my phone.

A guy is the last thing I need right now. This is *get-Jamie's-shit-together* time, not boy time. Maybe in a few months when I feel more settled, but not now. I feel as if I am back for a reason, and I need to be focused on that.

I increase my pace so my body doesn't have the energy to think about any of the boys that are currently tormenting me.

I arrive at the waterfall, my destination, in record-time. It doesn't have a name, as this trail isn't even on any map, but it's a local secret and the perfect place to get away from it all.

Sweaty and hot from the trip, I decide to cool off in the water. The pool below the waterfall isn't deep enough to swim in, but you can get under the spray of the cascading falls. After I undress, I wade in. It's cold but the hot sun offsets it. As I approach the stream of water, I stick my head under it, letting the icy water spill over my shoulders as I hope it melts the tension away.

This has been one of my favorite spots since I was little. One of the only times I remember doing something with my brother was when he brought me here. Now, I only come here to remember him and forget everything else. We may not have been close, but he was still my brother and I never really got a chance to get to know him.

I do remember idolizing him. Who doesn't idolize their older sibling? He was on the thin and lanky side, but I remember thinking he was so strong. He would pick me up and hold me upside down by my ankles. He had the coolest green eyes and reddish blonde hair. I was always jealous of his unique look. Tons of people have blue eyes, but not many have green.

He was the spitting image of my father. I know my mom is constantly reminded of the son she lost when she sees my father. She never even had a body to bury. He has a headstone in the graveyard, but the ground underneath holds an empty casket.

I step out from under the water and catch something out of the corner of my eye. I blink a few times, not believing what I am seeing. A shot of adrenalin shoots through me.

A wolf stands at the edge of the water, watching me.

Shit. My skin prickles with goosebumps.

I look around to find something to scare it off with and notice a stick on the opposite bank. I wade over and grab it, then return my attention to the wolf. His coat is solid black with a small white spot on his forehead. And he is huge. I know wolves are not supposed to be small, but he seems larger than I expected. Probably because I am less than twenty feet away.

We stay this way for a long time, staring into each other's eyes. His yellow eyes are a shocking contrast to his black fur.

The wolf shakes his head. What a strange thing for an animal to do. Then he slowly starts backing away. Once he is about fifty feet away, he turns around for one last look, then takes off running.

Holy fuck. I just had a staring contest with a wolf.

As the adrenaline from the encounter starts to wear off, I start to shiver. I realize the sun has gone behind the trees. It must be getting late.

I cautiously wade out of the pool and return to my clothes. Dressing quickly, I never take my eye off the direction that the wolf ran off in. Before leaving, I find a better stick to defend myself with. It may not be much, but I have a four-mile hike back to the car in the descending darkness and it's better than nothing.

Using a quick pace, I head back down the trail to get to my car. In my haste to get back, I step on a rock wrong and roll my ankle, bad. I let out a cry and fall to the ground.

I chide myself for not going home and getting my hiking boots before I went out. All I could think about was getting away, clearing my head, but I know better than to go hiking unprepared like this.

I stand up. It hurts, but I can walk. As I hobble down the path, I pull my phone from my pocket. No service. I never texted anyone to tell them where I was going. Well, double fuck.

I brought a bottle of water, but it's mostly empty. Using the stick as a cane, I slowly begin to make my way down the trail.

Using my internal gage, I would say I've already gone a mile, so I only have three more to go. But it's slow going. I continue down the path, keeping my eyes and ears peeled for any sign of the wolf. My dad is going to freak out at me for being out here alone. Especially after Jacob.

An hour later, it's almost dark, and now *I'm* freaking out.

There's no doubt about it now. I'm not going to make it back to my car before it's completely black outside.

Through the trees to my right, I spy a large rocky outcropping a few hundred feet in the distance. If I climb up on the rocks, I might be able to get service. I'll never hear the end of how irresponsible I am, but I think my ankle is hurt worse than I originally thought and I need help.

I reach the top of the rock just as the last rays of sunlight disappear.

I pull my phone out and almost cry when I see the bars. Quickly, I dial my dad. He will know where I am and how to find me.

He answers in a worried voice. "Jamie, where are you?"

Tears start falling down my face. It's so good to hear his voice. "Dad! I went hiking to clear my head and I rolled my ankle really bad . . ." Just as I am about to tell him where I am, the phone clicks. I pull it away from my ear. The display is dead.

Can I not catch a break?

At least I was able to get out that I went hiking. He knows that this is one of my favorite places, so hopefully he will come looking for me.

Carefully, I climb down the rock. It is so dark out and the moon is just a sliver.

I make my way back in the direction of the trail. After about two hundred feet, the ground starts to slope downward. Ugh, I must have climbed off the wrong side of the rock!

I look behind me, trying to see the rock, but I can't make out anything.

Well great, Jamie, now you lost the trail.

Suddenly, a loud howl pierces the air.

I am so fucked.

Chapter 11:

I'm cold, tired, and scared. I messed up big time and now I am lost in the forest, alone, in the middle of the night. Sitting with my back against a rock, legs pulled in for warmth, I curse my stupidity. I know better than this, yet here I am. Hurt, exhausted, and thirsty; oh, and did I mention I'm lost in the freaking forest. If my brain wasn't so distracted by stupid *boys*, this never would have happened.

After another hour of wandering around, trying to find the trail or the rocky outcropping, or anything else that looks familiar, I give up. I'm probably just getting myself more lost. With the minimal light from the moon and stars and the thick trees overhead, I can barely see anything.

I find a place where my back is protected, a rock I can lean against, and hunker down, shivering. I will save my energy for the morning when I can at least see. After my call to my dad, he probably has half the town looking for me, but it's still a long shot. Rocky Mountain National Park is huge. They don't know which trail I am on, and my car is not on a road where anyone will pass it.

Tomorrow I'll get myself back to my car and into town. For now, I'm just going to try and get some sleep.

As I lay on the cold forest floor, I promise myself that if I ever get out of this, I'm swearing off all boys for the time being.

Warmth.

I am engulfed in heat. I'm moving. Someone or something is moving me. My brain registers footsteps as each one jostles my body. Someone is carrying me.

The warmth is so nice, and I'm so exhausted, I feel myself drift off again.

There is sun shining in my eyes when I open them. Blinking a few times, I try to take in my surroundings. I still feel the warmth and realize I'm being carried; it wasn't a dream. I look up and see Wren's face. My movement alerts him that I am awake.

He pauses and sets me down on the ground. The warmth retreats, but I notice that I have a large jacket draped over my shoulders. Wren is in a black t-shirt and jeans. How does he always look so good? He must have given me his jacket. It may be summer, but, at this altitude, the temperature drops into the 40's most nights.

He squats down and looks at me with those eyes I'm obsessed with. "What the fuck were you thinking?"

The anger in his voice shocks me. I knew I would be getting some shit for this, but I expected sympathy first. Like, *are you all right, are you warm enough?*

He stands up and pulls water out of a backpack I hadn't noticed before. He tosses it at me and says, "Drink."

Seriously, what is his problem?

I take the water and take a gulp. Not because he told me to but because I'm thirsty.

After I down the full bottle, I look up at the now-pacing Wren. "How did you find me?"

Not that I am not grateful. I'm extremely happy that I'm not going to die alone in the woods. But, how did he know where I was?

"Last night, after you called your dad, he told everyone he knew to look for you. He named a few of your favorite trails. This was one of them."

I look around. If so many people are looking for me, *where is everyone else?*

As I suspected, my moment of stupidity is not going to just slide under the rug. Everyone is going to know, and I am never going to outlive this. Tourists get lost. Tourists get hurt. Locals are supposed to know better.

I broke all the basic rules when I went out hiking alone, without telling anyone where I was going, and taking nothing with me in case of an accident.

As if he can read my mind, he says, "We should be meeting up with the others soon. I was ahead of everyone."

I feel like he isn't telling me something.

Before I can ask him more, a voice I recognize as my dad's calls out. Wren yells back and in a few minutes, he comes running through the trees to get over to me.

I stand as he pulls me into a hug, "God, Jamie, you had me so worried. I'm so glad Wren found you. His tracking skills are incredible."

My dad holds me tight to his chest. The gravity of the situation finally hits home, and tears start to stream down my face. My dad continues to comfort me.

After a few minutes, he holds me out at arm's length. "You mentioned you were hurt? Can you walk?"

Up until this point, I hadn't been putting any weight on my ankle. I test it and cringe in pain. "Not looking good for walking out of here."

Before he can answer, Wren comes up behind me and scoops me up so fast, all the air whooshes out of my lungs. I blush. As I am cradled in his arms, he turns to my father and says, "I've got her."

The warmth of his chest radiates into me as he walks, and my dad follows, absolutely silent.

———

We were close to the trailhead when we met up with my

dad. When we get back to my car, there is a group of close to twenty people, most of them familiar faces. I thank everyone for helping to find me and apologize for being stupid.

Everyone seems very understanding. A few tell me stories about mistakes they made when they went out hiking. Everyone seems happy that I've been found all right, except Wren. When I look up, he's off on his own, scowling about something.

As the crowd disperses, he finally comes to me. "Let me drive you. You can't do it with that ankle."

My dad shakes his head. "Give him your keys, Jamie." He looks at Wren. "You can drive her car back to our house, but she's coming with me. She needs to go to the hospital to get that ankle looked at."

I start to protest, but he gives me a look that makes it die in my throat. "Okay."

Wren jumps in my car and drives off without another look at me. As we head back toward town, I use my dad's phone to call Mom. She answers on the first ring. "Jim! Did you find her? Is she all right?"

"Hey Mom, I'm fine."

For the next minute, she rattles off all sorts of worries.

"Mom, I'm fine, really. A little hungry and tired, but other than a twisted ankle, I am fine. That's why I am calling. Can you convince Dad not to take me to the hospital? I'm already embarrassed enough."

"Well, I'm glad you're all right, but I think it would be

best to be seen by a doctor. Dr. Frey is free this afternoon if you want to come here. That way I can see for myself that you are all right. Jamie, you had us all so worried!"

My dad must overhear the conversation, because he makes a U-turn and changes his route to my mom's office.

Ten minutes later, she comes rushing out of her office building and pulls me into a hug. "I'm so glad you're okay, but we both know you know better than that! What were you thinking?"

"I wasn't, that was the problem." By this point, my dad has gotten out of the car and is standing next to us.

He leans in and kisses my mom on the cheek. "We were really lucky to have Wren's help. He found her. That boy can track anything."

My mother replies, "We will have to have him over for dinner again. I'm so grateful that he helped find my baby girl. I don't know what I would do if I lost you, too."

Now I feel extra horrible. My parents have already been through so much with my brother. I shouldn't be putting myself at risk.

Turning to my parents, I say, "I can promise I learned my lesson loud and clear. I will be a lot more careful in the future."

With that, we head inside my mom's office so I can be looked over.

My thoughts drift back to Wren. Something about him is different, but I can't place my finger on it.

Chapter 12:

Finally, we arrive back at the house. It's only 10 am, but I am spent. I don't even have the energy to shower. Instead, I climb into bed and fall asleep.

I'm back in the forest, but this time the moon is bright enough that I can see my surroundings. I look up. A full moon is floating in the sky above.

Branches crack behind me and I spin around. It's the black wolf. His yellow eyes glow in the moonlight. His hot breath is on my face and I realize I am sitting on the ground.

I should be terrified, but I'm not. There is something about him that seems comforting. I feel the inexplicable urge to reach out and touch him. My hand lightly connects with the top of his head and I run it along the fur. It's so soft.

Another howl pierces the air, and he pulls away and looks in the direction it comes from. A low growl leaves his throat and his ears pull back.

I shoot up in bed, my heart beating fast.

What was that? It seemed too real to be a dream, but it must have been. I look at the clock. 4pm. I've slept most of the day.

Easing to my feet, I hobble to the bathroom and slip off the splint to take a shower. Under the spray of water, I think about my dream and the wolf. It felt so real; it sends chills down my back.

It wasn't the black wolf that scared me, but the howl that echoed through the forest. Something about it made all the hair on my body stand up. I don't know why, but I think it came from something that wanted to hurt me.

Dressed in sweats and a baggy t-shirt, I go downstairs to the kitchen. I freeze.

Wren is sitting at the bar, talking to my mom. Why can't I seem to get away from him? Do I even want to?

Yes. I am going to stick firm to my No Boys rule.

When my phone turned back on, I had a call and two texts from Liam. I deleted all of them unopened. I need Jamie time right now and I don't need him twisting my brain any further.

Wren is just staring at me. Why does he always do that?

My mom stands up and comes over. "You look better honey. How are you feeling?"

"I'm starving."

She walks over to the stove and stirs a pot. "Well, let's get you fed. The food should be ready in ten minutes." She turns to Wren. "Are you able to stay for dinner? We would love to have you."

Speak for yourself. But I try to keep the snarl off my face. He did help save me this morning. I should be grateful.

He looks intently at my face, as if reading my mind. "Janet, that would be great, if you don't mind having me."

"Of course not, dear. It's no problem!"

I look down at my clothes and get the urge to go change into something nicer since Wren is here. *No, Jamie, you don't care, because you have sworn off boys.*

Limping over to the bar, I sit in the chair next to Wren. Intentionally ignoring him, I ask my mom, "What's for dinner?"

It smells delicious and my stomach is rumbling. My dad gave me a protein bar he had in his car when we were heading to the doctor's office, but I fell asleep before I could eat anything else when we got home.

"Your dad decided it would be a good day for ribs. He knows they are one of your favorites. I'm just heating up the beans and I made potato salad with red potatoes just how you like it. And, I made brownies for dessert."

My stomach rumbles so loud people on the other side of the world can hear it. I clamp a hand over it and blush.

"I'll take that as a sign that you are happy?"

I nod.

To my surprise, Mark stops by after dinner to check on me.

"Hey," he says when I answer the door and lead him into the living room. "I'm sorry I couldn't be there. I was busy . . ." Mark stops when he sees Wren. The two eye each other suspiciously. "Are you busy?"

"No! Not at all!" I say brightly. "This is Wren. He's one of my father's rangers."

"He was a great help to us, finding Jamie," my mother says.

Mark sizes him up. "Were you?"

Wren's shrug is humble, but his smirk is otherwise.

I remind myself, *no boys!* and try to ignore their male posturing. My mom offers Mark leftovers from dinner and goes into the kitchen to help him, leaving me in the living room with Wren.

He looks unhappy, even more so than ordinary. As a man of few words he doesn't say anything, so I ask, "What's up?"

He just keeps staring at me, saying nothing.

"Seriously, what is your problem?"

Half the time I want to jump his bones and the other half I want to punch him in the face. Nobody has ever been able to piss me off so easily before.

"Are you and him back together?"

Him? It takes me a second to realize he is talking about Mark. Why would he think that?

"It's none of your business, but no we are not. We are

friends, or I hope we are heading in that direction. I messed up big time, and I don't know if he has forgiven me yet."

With that, he stands up. He takes a step closer, eyes trained on my lips. Is he planning on kissing me? I scoot back and put my hands up.

"Oh no you don't. No more crazy kisses right before you walk out the door. No more kisses in general. I need me time, no boys allowed."

He lets out a harrumph and stalks to the door. He mumbles something under his breath that sounds like, "You will be mine soon." I don't have time to argue because in the next second, he's gone. Besides, maybe my brain was just making it up.

Before I can think about it, Mark returns with a plate of food and a huge smile on his face. "I forgot how good your mom's cooking is. So much better than the frozen pizza I was planning on having when I got home."

For the next hour, we make small talk and watch a movie. It feels nice hanging out with Mark again. Even with the underlying tension, I forgot how well we exist together. I'm not worried about what I'm going to say or how I look. It doesn't matter with him. We've known each other so long that we just are, and it works.

Unlike my time with Wren, who twists me in knots and throws me constant curveballs.

Jamie, stop. No boys!

Chapter 13:

Because of my ankle, I spend the week reading and watching TV. At first it was nice and relaxing, but now I am ready to get out of the house and do something. I text Tollen and, to my surprise, she doesn't ignore me. We agree to meet up this afternoon at her house to hang out.

I'm equal parts nervous and excited. During college, I had other female friends, but none as close as I was with Tollen. I really need a girlfriend right now with everything swirling through my head. Mark will be off limits, but he is the least of my problems.

As I am getting ready to head out the door, my mom walks in from work. "Hey honey, where are you off to? Are you ready to be out and about?"

My little adventure in the woods really seemed to scare my mom. She hasn't been this clingy since my brother died. I have tried to be understanding since I can't even imagine what it is like to lose a child, but I am feeling suffocated. I'm twenty-five, not eight, and I don't want to stay locked away in the house forever.

"Heading over to Tollen's for a few hours. Don't worry, I will take it easy!"

With that, I move quickly out to my car. My mom won't make me stay, but if she gives me the guilty face, I am doomed.

When I arrive at Tollen's, I'm even more nervous. I was so stupid for ignoring her all those years. I want my best friend back, if she will take me.

She is outside on the bench under the trellis, wearing shorts and a tank top, soaking up the warm summer sun. Toby is on a blanket at her feet, playing with toys. Toby has a floppy sun hat and too much sunscreen on her face.

As I get out of my car, Tollen waves. I wave back as I go through the white gate. As soon as I walk into the yard, Toby stands up and runs over to me to hug my leg. I'm shocked and don't know what to do.

She turns her huge blue eyes up on me and smiles as she says, "J . . . e," her version of my name, and then throws her hands up like she wants me to pick her up. I oblige, lifting her little body into my arms.

I notice that her clothes match her mom's and I chuckle because it is such a Tollen thing to do. Growing up, she always wanted to be a fashion designer and was constantly trying new clothing combinations to make a statement. That all ended her junior year when she visited NYC. She spent the next year telling me how awful and dirty it was and how there was no way she'd ever live there.

Holding Toby in one arm and a bag of wine and cookies in the other I say, "Hey."

Her face seems uncertain. "I see my daughter has taken a liking to you. She wouldn't stop talking about breakfast the other morning and how you also got the Mickey Mouse pancakes then moved the fruit around to make a smiley face."

I was very hungover. Funny, I barely remember it.

"She is an adorable little girl." I've always wanted kids, but later in my life. The plan was to get my career set first. But the more I hang out with Toby, the more I think "later" is "now". Maybe my hormones are going crazy and that's why I'm having so many boy issues.

I hold out the bag to her. "I brought wine and cookies, girl day essentials."

After I say the word cookie, the three-year-old in my arms starts bouncing and saying, "Ooki, ooki."

We both laugh and Tollen motions for me to follow her into the house. "Let's get Toby her cookie and us some wine then head back outside. It's such a nice day. I don't want to be cooped up inside."

I nod in agreement.

After we are back outside and situated, I look around at her beautiful garden and start the conversation by asking about it.

Tollen replies, "It was pretty nice when I bought the

house, but it inspired me to get more into gardening. I find it relaxing and it is so beautiful when they are all blooming."

"Well, you have done a great job. I love it! I tried to have plants, but I can't even seem to keep a succulent alive."

At this, we both start laughing. We stick with light subjects as we drink our wine and watch Toby play. Slowly, the walls between us come down.

Feeling like we are making a little headway back into being friends, I decide to dive into the topic I really need advice on — boys.

"Tollen, how would you feel about helping me with some guy advice?"

She tenses slightly, but she has no reason to. I'm not planning on asking about Mark. But maybe I should? I can't get a read on what, if anything, is going on between them.

"What are your thoughts on Wren? Have you met him?"

She takes a sip of her wine as she thinks. "Well, he is ruggedly gorgeous. Have you seen those eyes? But, to be honest, I don't think I've ever talked to him. Mark said he found you in the forest?"

I nod, remembering the warmth of his arms as he carried me out of the forest.

Tollen continues before I can say anything. "You were an idiot, but I am glad you ended up being okay. We both know that situation could have turned out a lot differently. I never did get the full story."

I quickly fill her in on the call from Liam, and how I was

so twisted, I wasn't thinking.

The only thing I leave out is my encounter with the wolf. For whatever reason, I haven't told anyone about it. My only reasoning is that part of me feels like it's a secret I shouldn't share.

After I tell Tollen the whole story, she just stares at me for a moment.

"Wow. Let me rephrase that. You were damn lucky Wren found you so quick or it could have been a whole lot worse. Did he ever tell you how he found you? That trail's really dangerous, even in broad daylight."

I shake my head. "No, he never went into details, but I've wondered the same thing."

"From what you're telling me, he seems fond of you. From what I have heard, he is quiet and keeps to himself. One of the other girls that works at the art gallery asked him out once. Said he seemed uncomfortable the whole time. Like he was too good to be spending his time that way. The word is that he was an Academy kid back when we were in high school, and they always thought they were better than everyone else. Remember that party?"

I nod.

"There is something about him that doesn't seem quite right. I would be careful if I were you."

She says the same thing I have been thinking. He does seem strange. Maybe the desire I feel towards him is solely from his looks, since he's very easy on the eyes. I haven't seen him with his shirt off, but when he carried me, I felt the muscle definition of his chest.

A hand waves in front of my face and I look up at Tollen, embarrassed. She smiles as if she can see where my brain went.

Tollen reaches out for my now empty glass as she says, "Let's refill and then I want to hear more about this boss of yours. That sounds like a story."

With a new full glass of wine in my hand, I dive into the subject of Liam. As I tell her the story, I realize just how one-sided it was. There were so many red flags.

"Tollen, I feel so embarrassed. He was using me, and I fell for him. He was my boss. I never should have gone there in the first place. Look where it got me. He was probably with other women the whole time we were together. Or *not* together together, but you know."

I look over at Toby, who is playing with her toy blocks. She has some chocolate smeared on her face, along with a look of concentration as she tries to build a block tower.

Tollen must understand what I am thinking. "She is still young enough that you can say whatever you want. But I do need to start watching my mouth. She said 'shit' the other day and we both know Mark rarely uses colorful language, so she must have learned it from me."

I nod. "It seems obvious now that he was using me. But now he keeps calling and texting me. I figured he would forget about me and move onto the next girl but now, I'm confused."

Mulling it over, Tollen says, "From the sound of it, you seem to care about him. Maybe it's not the big L, but you were together for what almost two years?" I nod and she continues, "I'd say you are always going to wonder what his intentions were if you never talk to him again. Take it from someone that has been on the ignored side… it's not fun."

Just as I'm about to apologize for the hundredth time, a police patrol car comes flying up the road and skids to a stop. Mark hops out, concern on his face. When he sees us, he visibly relaxes and slows his pace toward us.

As he's opening the gate, Toby sees him and runs over. "Dada, Dada."

He swoops her up and holds her tight he says, "Why aren't either of you answering your phones?" His voice is tense.

I pat my pocket and realize I must have left my phone in the car. Tollen answers before I can. "We've just been catching up. I don't think either of us realized we didn't have our phones on us."

Mark wipes the chocolate from Toby's cheeks. He sets her down and says, "Tobs, why don't you go grab me one of whatever is smeared all over your face."

She takes her job very seriously and toddles into the house. Murmurs of "ookie" and "dada" come from her direction.

Mark is getting rid of her. My concern spikes.

"What's wrong?"

He takes a deep breath all right.

"There was a bear attack, or we think it was a bear attack,

on a pair of hikers, two young women. It was outside the park on the west side of town. I was just there, helping, for the last few hours.

"The bear did a number on the two girls and neither of them had identification on their person. I was worried it was you two and when you didn't answer my calls, I got even more worried. I called your house, Jamie, and your mom said you were hanging out with Tollen, making me even more concerned. I rushed over here as soon as I could."

We both ask a few more questions, but Mark can't share many details. The mood of our calm afternoon has been turned upside down. I tell Tollen I am going to head home as Mark follows her into her house.

As I get into my car, the thought of those poor women chills me to the bone. I am immediately thrown back to when my brother was attacked and killed. It's been a long time, but I wonder if what killed my brother killed those girls? They always thought it was a bear, but the whole situation was very hush hush. Even at ten years old I remember thinking people moved past it very fast.

An iciness travels down my spine as I remember the howl I heard when I was lost in the forest. Were both attacks done by the wolf? Was I in more danger than I thought the other night?

Chapter 14:

Over the next week, the bear attack is the talk of the town. There hasn't been a fatal animal attack since my brother and his friends seventeen years ago. Animals tend to mind their own business.

This week has been a constant reminder of my brother's death for all of us and it has been tough. I'm older now and I realize how much we don't know.

The two girls were identified when their parents reported them missing a few days after the incident. They were both college students from the city, up for a day of hiking. Every day rangers have been scouring the trail, trying to track down the bear so it can be euthanized. Once an animal kills, it can't stay alive. It's too dangerous. My father has been sullen and quiet, and I know he's having flashbacks. They never did find the animal that attacked my brother and his friends.

While I'm working at the shop, the bell above the door rings and Wren walks in. I haven't talked to him since he left my house in a huff after I rebuffed his advance. In his uniform, hiking boots, and a black shirt, he looks edible, like something I wouldn't be able to turn down this time.

He gives me a small smirk, like he can read my thoughts. I shake my head trying to think of anything else. No such luck.

He leans on the counter. I wait for him to say something, but he just stares at me. Again.

My patience breaks. "Hey, can I get you something to drink?"

Really, Jamie? That is the best you can think of?

"Coffee, black."

As I am getting him his coffee, I feel his eyes drilling into the back of my head.

Turning around, I hand him his coffee and ask, "Yes?"

He takes a sip of his coffee, "We got the bear."

It takes me a second to understand his words. They caught the bear that killed those girls.

"Well that's good to hear! I was getting worried that my father was going to get shot with all those people roaming the forest with guns."

He nods in agreement. He takes a seat at one of the tables closest to the coffee bar. Another customer comes in and I help them. Wren's eyes are on me the whole time, watching me while I work.

What is he still doing here?

After the other customer leaves, Wren sets his coffee on

the counter and comes around it. He stops super close to me, his eyes probing. I have to look away. "Um, you're not really supposed to be back here. Roberta—"

"Jamie, will you come over to my house tonight so I can cook dinner for you?"

I'm shocked. This seems so out of character for him. I know he wants to touch me, but he's being good, keeping his hands to himself. Probably because of how I acted the last time.

I glance up at him. He gets more gorgeous the closer I get. Not like Liam's pretty boy looks or Mark's warm teddy bear looks. He's rougher, but much more appealing.

I promised myself no boys, but what's wrong with a friendly dinner between friends?

"Yes, a friendly dinner sounds very nice. How does seven sound?" I am so lying to myself, but I am determined that this will be a meal between friends, nothing else.

Mark and Tollen seem to have grown closer since this incident so I haven't spent much time with them this week. I need to get out of the house; the tension is suffocating.

Wren's eyes burn with heat and the pull between us only increases as he stares at me.

The doorbell rings again causing him to step away. He murmurs, "Seven," then slips through the door without a backward glance, leaving his barely touched coffee on the counter.

What did I just get myself into?

Still flustered, I look at my next customer. The first thing I see is a blond mop of hair I would recognize anywhere.

Liam.

Chapter 15:

Liam is here. Standing in the coffee shop in my small town.

All the memories I have tried so hard to forget come crashing back. All the nights spent together, dinners out, and "breaks" in his office.

What is he doing here? How did he find me?

I haven't answered a single one of his texts or calls, thinking he'd get the picture.

Now he is here. Standing in front of me in tan shorts and a green polo that makes his eyes pop. He looks amazing, and, without my consent, my body reacts.

I square my shoulders. He was my boss, so he always seemed to have the upper hand in our relationship, or hook ups, whatever you want to call them. But no more.

"Hello, Liam, can I get you something to drink?"

"You never answered me. I called. I texted and called again and . . . nothing." He hides it well, but I can see some anger burning in his cool blue eyes. I know he isn't used to being ignored.

"I don't owe you anything, Liam. If I didn't want to talk to you then that was my choice." At that moment, a group of young girls comes through the door, giggling. They all seem to stop at the same time and stare at Liam.

I clear my throat to get their attention. Slowly, they pull their eyes away from him. Ignoring Liam, I get their orders, skim lattes with extra sugar syrup.

As they walk out the door, I turn back to Liam, who hasn't moved. "I'm working, Liam. What do you want?"

"Jamie, I have missed you. I know we didn't end things well and you probably hate me, but will you just hear me out?"

Liam is a shrewd businessman, who rarely shows much emotion. He doesn't compromise and he doesn't take no for an answer; he simply bulldozes everything in his way.

I will not be bulldozed by him, but the emotion flashing through his eyes makes me lessen my reaction. During the years we were together, I never saw that look.

I glance at the clock and sigh. "I'm off in twenty. If you want to wait, we can talk."

His eyes brighten slightly. "I'm staying at the Stanford hotel. We could have dinner there."

This was how our entire relationship, if it can be called that, went. He would just say what we were doing, and I would go along with it. Not anymore. I don't know where this may lead, but he is not going to dictate everything like he did last time.

Plus, going to his hotel will likely lead to more than dinner and I'm smarter than that.

Not to mention Wren, who invited me over to dinner tonight. It may be as friends, but I decide to mess with Liam a little. He put me through hell and it's time he got some of his own medicine.

"I'm busy tonight. I already have a dinner date," I say, not hiding my delight in the way his eyes show a flash of anger. Were his eyes always this transparent and I just never noticed? "But we should talk. There is a table out back if you want to wait."

He looks shocked that I said no to his plan. Good.

After ordering an iced macchiato, he heads out back. I look at the clock. Ten minutes until I am done with my shift. What the hell am I going to say to him?

Roberta walks in a few minutes later. One look at my face and she can tell something is wrong. I give her a quick recap of the situation with Liam, and Roberta says, "You seem to have lingering feelings for him, so go and talk to him. He drove over an hour to come and see you. You were obviously more than just a quick lay. In my experience, guys' brains work very differently than ours. He may not have realized he cared until you were gone. My advice is to hear him out, but don't fall into an old routine that already didn't work once."

With her advice swirling through my head, I go out to the

back patio and find him talking on the phone. I realize it's the middle of the week and he likely interrupted his busy schedule to see me. How did he know where to find me, anyway?

He sees me and ends the call without saying anything. He stands and leans in to kiss me, but I turn my head to the side so his lips touch my cheek instead.

Before I can say anything, he grabs my shoulders and looks me straight in the eyes. "God Jamie, I've missed you like crazy. You have every right to be mad at me, I didn't handle things well. I thought I could forget and move on, but I couldn't. Something about you won't let me forget." He looks riled and confused, like he really can't understand why he can't get me out of his brain.

I take a step back.

"Liam, stop. I know what we had was not a relationship. I thought it was, but it never was one to you." Liam tries to interrupt but I stop him. "I thought I was in love with you and it hurt me when you dropped me without a second thought. It made me realize just how stupid I had been."

"No, Jamie. You're wrong. It was a relationship. I got freaked out when we got caught. And then you came back here—"

"Liam. Please. Let me get this out. I didn't run home because of you. I knew one day I would return, and it felt like it was time. Part of me is connected to this area. I tried to fight it for years, but since I have returned, I feel a level of peace I was never able to accomplish when I was gone.

"I am not proud of my actions when it comes to you. We both knew we were doomed to fail. I apologize for not returning your calls and texts, but I hadn't decided what to say yet.

"Yes, I am still attracted to you, but I am not just going to jump into bed with you because you drove all the way up here. I am not a pawn you can manipulate, not anymore. I must get home and change before my other plans for the night."

With that, I walk off the porch and to my car.

As I put my key into the ignition, I fully expect to never hear from him again. He was with a version of Jamie I never plan on being again. Maybe it's because of that night in the forest, but I feel like I've grown a new layer of skin.

I will not be treated poorly. I am better than that.

Chapter 16:

As I pull up in front of Wren's house, my stomach starts to somersault. I made it clear that this was a friendly dinner, but I already know I was lying to myself. It is as if my cells are pulling me toward him in a purely primal manner.

I hate being told what to do, so I immediately feel the need to rebel, even against my own body. Strange, I know, but I'm done apologizing for being myself.

As I walk to the door, bottle of wine in my hand, I remind myself that the point of tonight is to get to know Wren. Even though we have interacted a fair amount since I've returned, I know very little about him.

I raise my hand to knock on the door, but it opens before I have the chance. Wren is in the doorway, an expression on his face that brings only one word to my mind: dangerous. In black jeans, black boots, and a tight black t-shirt, he screams rebel. It's such a contrast to the preppy, country club clothes Liam wore earlier.

He says nothing as he turns and walks back into the house. No hey, how're you doing, nothing. So much for a *friendly* dinner.

Stepping inside, I shut the door behind myself, peek in the mirror by the door, and follow.

I spent longer than I would like to admit getting dressed for tonight. For a friendly dinner, I should have worn jeans, but I instead chose a flowy, blue summer dress that probably looks like I've made too much effort. I curled my hair, giving the traditionally straight strains some volume and took my time trying to make my makeup look natural. I wanted to look nice but not like I took too much time getting ready.

Why do I get so nervous around Wren?

Every cell in my body comes alive as I enter the kitchen and see him standing out on a balcony beyond the sliding glass doors. He doesn't turn as I come up behind him and stand at the railing beside him, looking out over the town below and the mountains in the backdrop.

This makes me think of the view I had from my old apartment in the city. It faced the side of another building. I always forgot to close the blinds as I walked around and found my neighbors staring. But here, on this hillside overlooking Accalia, there are no other houses close enough. We are completely alone.

But this is just a friendly dinner. A dinner to get to know Wren. I have a thousand questions about him after all, the least of them being how he can afford a place as huge as this on a ranger's salary. I turn to him, ready to get some answers.

But he moves so fast I can barely breathe as he cages me against the railing with his arms and presses his body against mine.

All my thoughts disappear as the heat of his body sears mine, sparking wherever our bodies touch. I look into his eyes and find them more yellow than brown. My brain cycles back, picking up a thread of déjà vu, but loses it as he lifts a hand to trail it down the side of my face. His pupils are dilated, his breathing heavy.

In my brain, I keep chanting, *friends, friends, friends.*

But I also know I'm so screwed.

As if he can read my thoughts, he asks, "Why are you trying to stop this? I can tell you are as affected by me as I am by you."

Why am I fighting this? It feels so right when I think about taking that next step, giving over to my body's demands to be with him. I've never felt an attraction like this before. The intensity frightens me a little.

I have a habit of diving in too fast and end up getting burned, and I don't want that to happen again. These feelings I have unsettle me, causing a battle in my brain as if two people are arguing over what to do.

"We don't even know each other." Having his body this close frays my nerves and my willpower. My body is getting more demanding the longer I stay pressed against him.

"We know each other better than you think. Jamie, I can't

get you out of my head."

We know each other? I just met him a few weeks ago.

I slowly slide out from between his arms. I know he could easily stop me, but he doesn't try.

"Does this pull between us not concern you? I feel as if something is pushing us together and I don't like my life being dictated by anyone other than me. I need wine. Where is your corkscrew?"

Wren chuckles. Mr. Serious is laughing.

"What's so funny?"

Wren walks by on his way to the kitchen, brushing his body against mine. I think intentionally. "Your dad always talks about his stubborn daughter. Apparently, it extends to destiny's plan as well."

Destiny's plan? Wren had better start talking because I always feel he knows information that I am not privy to.

As I walk inside, Wren opens the bottle of wine and pours two glasses.

He hands me mine and motions in the direction of the living room. "Since you seem to want to talk so much, let's go sit and talk."

Wine in hand, I nod and follow him to the sofa, determined to get some of my questions answered. I start simple. "Why do you live here? How can you live here?" I motion with my hands to the house he lives in.

Wren readjusts so that his calf brushes against mine. "Why are you questioning me so much? Do you interrogate everyone you want to sleep with?"

The sip of wine I had just taken sputters gracelessly out of my mouth. Who does he think he is? Trying to gain some composure, I wipe my chin and say, "Maybe I just know nothing about you. I like to know stuff about my friends. We are friends, right?"

No, I'm not letting this go, so you'd better answer.

He harrumphs and shrugs. "I don't really like talking about myself, but since you just won't drop it, I'll see if I can please you." He leans back with his glass of wine.

"I moved back up here two years ago, and work with your father to help track and tag animals in the park. To answer the other question you haven't asked yet, yes, that's how I found you in the forest. Your movements left a very clear path.

"When I have time, I help out at The Academy when they need me. And I had an uncle, who took me in when my parents died. They all had money—quite a bit of it—and now it's mine."

Wren stares straight ahead, that same serious expression on his face, but now it seems even more so. *Great Jamie, you dug until he answered and now you have upset him. Why are you like this?*

"Oh." I don't know what else to say. I notice his wine glass is empty, so I start to stand so I can fill it.

Suddenly, Wren grabs my arm. "Where are you going?" His eyes are almost panicked.

"I was just going to go get more wine."

He slowly releases my arm and lets me go. In a daze, I head to the kitchen and pour two more glasses. There is a lot more going on in Wren's head than he likes people to see.

When I return, I sit next to him on the couch and hand him his glass.

"You told me about yourself, so it's only fair I tell you stuff about me. I—"

"I know."

I stare at him. "What?"

"Your father. He told me."

"Oh, right."

He suddenly reaches over and grabs my hand, "I'm sorry to hear about your brother. Just remember sometimes things aren't as black and white as they appear."

A little strange. My father told Wren about Jacob? He never talks about it to me. Never.

He makes slow, small circles on my arms as he drains his glass. I had more questions, but my mind goes blank as his finger continues to circle. I can't deny the attraction I have towards Wren. Who wouldn't be with a guy like him? But the pull seems deeper, more dangerous somehow.

I look over at his shaggy brown hair, broad shoulders, and nicely defined arms. I know how strong he is because he carried me for over a mile out of the forest. I remember the feeling of his hard chest against my body.

My heart rate increases, and my palms become sweaty. As if he can sense the change in me, he gazes straight into my eyes.

How can my body be pulling me towards him and sending out warning signals at the same time?

He sets his wine down, grabs mine, and puts it on the table next to him. He moves so I am caged below him on the couch. The warmth and pressure of his body melts against me, waking up the need I have been trying so hard to push down. His eyes are heavy and dark with desire.

His body vibrates with need and my own body begins to match it. He pauses, hovering over me, as if waiting for me to say it's okay. I try to sort through the fog in my brain. The *friends, friends, friends* chorus in my head is so weak now. There's a warning signal there, too, but my body doesn't seem to care.

He grinds himself into me and I can feel how much he desires me.

What the hell, Jamie? It's just a hookup. Maybe it will even help to reduce the desire you feel for him.

All it takes is a small nod of my head and he closes the remaining distance between us. His lips connect with mine, shooting sparks through my body. My body molds perfectly to his. My desperation soon meets his and I press back with the same force he is giving.

I feel a slight nip from his teeth, and it drives me insane.

All thoughts are gone. There are only feelings now.

I need to feel him. I want to run my hands over his hard chest.

As I pull at Wren's shirt, it rips as I shred it off his body. My hands start to explore as my lips continue to stay busy with his.

His hands move below my dress, feeling and pleasuring as they go.

He pulls back and I feel cold without his touch. "Jamie, there are things I need to tell you ..."

I cut him off with my mouth and murmur into his lips, "We can talk later, I need you now."

He rips my dress open, buttons flying everywhere as I'm exposed. My need intensifies and I yank at his pants. He kicks them off and dives back into the kiss.

I'm on fire as the pleasure ripples through my body. The last barrier of clothing disappears, and we come together. We are one, meshed together. It's fast and hard and an overwhelming need pools in my stomach.

As I begin to soar over the edge, I feel Wren tense, ready to follow. The intensity increases until I can't stay quiet. I scream and moan. We lie together, breathing heavy and still reveling in the ecstasy.

There has only been one other time where I have felt intensity like this. The Academy boy from high school.

My thoughts are soon forgotten as Wren's mouth finds my breast and I feel him harden inside me. His words are much calmer than I'm feeling as he says, "Why don't we continue this in the bedroom?"

Still at loss for words, I can only nod. I have never felt

better, and I never want to stop.

Cradled in his arms, he carries me down the hallway. I stare at his lips and can't help myself from taking a taste.

His lips press back against mine as he deepens the kiss. Wren presses me up against a cold wall. Needing more, I position myself to take him inside me.

Like an animal let out of its cage, he takes me again, my back sliding against the rough wall. My hands roam as if they want to memorize every inch of his body. Locked together, I feel right. I feel at home. What is this man doing to me?

He drives harder taking me over the edge.

As I refocus, I look into Wren's eyes and swear they are glowing. They make me think of the wolf from the forest.

My need returns and my thoughts return to now. I have just had two rounds of the most mind-blowing sex of my life, yet I crave more.

One breathy word comes out of my mouth. "Bedroom."

Wren obliges and all but runs the rest of the way. I don't get a look at the room as my mouth returns to his.

The softness of the bed connects with my back, which is still raw from the wall. My desire hasn't died, it's only grown. Every inch of my body craves Wren and his feelings seem to match.

Dinner is forgotten and so is that voice inside me. That silly little voice that only wanted *friends*.

Chapter 17:

Yes, the plan was to have a friendly dinner, but damn if that wasn't the best sex I have ever had. The intensity, the passion, the fire that wouldn't die. I lost track of the amount of times we came together. As the first signs of dawn entered the sky, I finally drifted off to sleep.

I look over at a Wren now, sleeping next to me. His face looks so peaceful, and I wonder what he is dreaming about. He always has a shield up, but in sleep he looks like he has found the peace that he hasn't been able to achieve while awake.

I take in the room I didn't get a chance to see last night. A wall of windows frames the continental divide's snow-capped peaks. The giant room is sparsely furnished, dominated by the massive king bed we are on. A black chair in the corner with a reading light is the only other piece of furniture. The colors are dark and neutral, making me feel as if I'm a part of the forest, surrounded by trees.

My shifting alerts Wren that I am awake. He rolls over and grabs me. I'm instantly soothed as his heat engulfs me. Entrapped in his arms, a smile pulls at my lips.

What was I so worried about? Why was I fighting so hard to stay away?

Light kisses trail down my neck. My body begins to stir again as his hand draws slow circles on my hip.

His voice still full of sleep, Wren says, "God, you are amazing. I knew it would be amazing, but that was so much better than last time. I've never stopped thinking about you."

Last time? What is he talking about? The kiss we shared in the parking lot the other night?

"What do you mean, last time?"

"It was like we were tearing at each other because we couldn't control ourselves. I never forgot."

My blood instantly chills. The Academy party. The random guy. It was Wren.

Every hair on my body stands on end. I have never been able to explain that night, half believing I made it up. He just left me. Without a word. And I thought I was pregnant.

Oh, God. I should have listened to the voice in my head and stayed away. So many of the things he said make so much more sense now. He has been waiting for me, knowing exactly who I was.

I need to get out of here. I don't trust my body to think and act normally around him.

I jump off the bed and make it out of the bedroom before

he realizes what is happening. I grab my phone and keys from the kitchen counter where I left them, when I planned to have a nice friendly dinner.

What a joke. How could I have been so stupid?

In the living room, I look for my dress and find it under the coffee table, in shreds. Shit.

Wren yells my name, his feet pounding on the floor. I don't want to talk to him. I find a discarded sweatshirt on a chair and pull it over my head. Leaving my shoes, I rush to my car as quickly as I can.

Key in the ignition, I start the car and peel out of his driveway. Barefoot and wearing his oversized sweatshirt.

After I've made it a few miles, I pull over on the side of the road and let the tears flow. The Academy party in high school was the craziest and strangest night of my life. I have tried to push it down but part of me has always come back to it.

After I pull myself together, I almost laugh. No matter what I do, I can't seem to get my shit together. Craziness just seems to follow me wherever I go.

I can't go home like this. It must be around noon and I can't risk one of my parents being home. I may be a grown woman, but they'd kill me if they saw me like this. My dad would probably grab his shotgun and head to Wren's house, demanding to know why his daughter came home so distraught.

And why am I so upset? Last night was seriously amazing.

I've always felt that strange pull to Wren, so shouldn't I be happy that there is only one guy out there that this seems to happen with, not two?

Why did he run away then? And will he do it again? He is hiding much more than this. Maybe it's good that I got out of there as quickly as I did. I need to keep my distance from him. He is only going to cause trouble.

As if she can sense my dilemma, Tollen's name pop ups on my phone. I lift it to my ear, my voice cracking. "Hey Tollen! Please tell me you are home?"

She takes a second before she starts talking. "Yes, I am, and Mark has Toby, so I was going to see if you wanted to do something since I know you're off today. Is everything all right?"

Not wanting to get into it over the phone, I say, "No. But I'll be there in ten. Please tell me you have champagne in your house. It's a mimosa kind of morning."

As I pull up to her house, I look around to see if anyone is around, then hop out of my car and run up to the door. I knock loudly and slip inside the instant she opens it.

She takes one look at me. "What the hell have you been up to?"

I reply, "Drinks first, then I will tell you everything."

An hour later, the bottle of champagne is empty and I've told her every detail. Including the night in high school. It sounds so bad when I say it out loud. I'm so embarrassed.

She doesn't say a word the entire time I spill my story.

Finally, she leans over and puts a hand on my leg. "First off, there is nothing wrong with you. We are young women and there is nothing wrong with being attracted to or sleeping with men. Especially men that look as good at Wren does. I'm sure he is hiding a very handsome body underneath those clothes."

I nod because she is right about that. My mind drifts back to his muscled chest and the unique tattoo of a compass he has on his upper chest.

"I was always jealous of you in high school. You seemed to have it all figured out. A great guy, a plan, and drive to make whatever you wanted happen. But I wonder if being attached to one guy for so long has sparked your recent guy issues?"

I stare at her, not quite sure what she is getting at.

"Hear me out. For all of high school, you were with Mark. He is an amazing guy, but that's our time to explore, try things out, mess up and learn from it. Believe me, I've made my fair number of mistakes, too. But you missed out on that. That night at the Academy party was a symptom of that. You were looking for a little adventure to spice things up."

Her words hit the nail right on the head. I have never come to this conclusion on my own, but as I think back over the last few years, I know she is right. There was a part of me that felt like I had missed out. Hadn't gotten the true teenage experience.

"And Jamie, as long as you were safe, there is no reason to

be worried about last night. It might be best to give yourself some space from him until you can determine your feelings. You never said you wanted to be with him, only that you felt pulled to him and desperate to be together. That doesn't sound like the making of anything that is going to turn out well.

"Not that I have any guys currently in my life, but if you want to hang out more to distract you, I'm your girl. I'm happy you're back. And I am starting to understand why you had to leave and couldn't keep any of the channels of communication open."

She is right. I need to stay away from Wren. Or at least not be alone with him. I can't trust myself around him.

At that moment, my phone dings with a text from Liam.

Draining the last of my mimosa I ask, "What do you think I should do about Liam?"

Tollen looks me up and down. "Well, you can't go anywhere like that. Let's see if we can find anything in my closet that will fit you. And a shower may be a good idea. You smell like sex."

I don't know why, but her last words are so funny, and I break down laughing as reality hits me. Tollen joins in and soon we are both in hysterics.

Getting myself under control, I say, "All those nights we talked about our futures, we never imagined anything like this, did we?"

I fall into another fit of giggles as I look over at my best friend. How did I survive seven years without her?

I didn't.

Chapter 18:

As I walk into the lobby of the Stanford hotel, the nicest hotel in our small town, I look around for Liam.

Tollen convinced me to at least meet with him and hear him out. Yes, the way our relationship started and then ended was extremely rocky, but he drove all this way. I feel like he at least deserves a chance to explain himself. Plus, it will be a nice distraction from Wren.

Whatever happens, I plan to take it slow. If it's worth having, then it's worth taking the time to grow it. Time to see if I can handle a responsible adult conversation.

Liam is standing by a table in the middle of the room with a phone to his ear. His blond hair is styled, he is clean shaven, and he is wearing a blue polo shirt and grey slacks. Even without the suit he typically wears to the office, his confidence is present every time he moves. He was born to be a CEO and he knows it.

When he sees me, he hangs up immediately and walks

over. I wonder who he just hung up on?

I can't help but compare him to Wren's wild and dangerous appeal. They're like two sides of a coin, complete opposites.

When he steps up to me, he kisses both of my cheeks in greeting, the same way he always used to, at least when we were outside of the office.

"Hello, Jamie, thank you for meeting me. I thought about your words and I don't blame you for being skeptical of me. I didn't treat you properly when we were together, and for that I am sorry. If you will give me the chance, I would like to start over."

He puts his hand out and says, "Hello, my name is Liam White. I'm a workaholic, but in my spare time I enjoy traveling, boating, and playing golf. I think you are very beautiful. Would you like to have dinner with me?"

Taking his hand, I follow his lead, "Hello, Liam, my name is Jamie Carter. I am currently working at a coffee shop while I am between jobs. I enjoy hiking, coffee, and books, among other things, and it would be my pleasure to have dinner with you."

Keeping my hand in his, he walks into the restaurant, only releasing my hand to pull out my chair.

I flash back to all the times we've done this before. But this feels different. Before, we didn't talk much. Both of us used dinner as a prelude to the later activities. This time, Liam asks lots of questions, mostly about my hometown.

I also learn a lot more about Liam. He has an older brother and a younger sister. He explains that Amtika is a subsidiary of his father's larger company, one that Liam built on his own.

After an hour, I know more about Liam than I learned in the years we were together. As we stand up to leave, I expect him to try to get me to come up to his room and am ready to shut him down. I don't know where this is heading, but we need to take it slow.

Instead, he shocks me by kissing my cheek. "What are you doing tomorrow?"

Tomorrow? I go through my mental calendar and realize tomorrow is Sunday. I have to work in the morning.

"I work until noon, but after that, I have no plans."

I expect him to invite me to another meal, but I'm surprised when he says, "I have heard the hiking around here is incredible. Would you want to show me one of your favorite trails?"

Hiking? He wants to go hiking?

I think about the attack that happened a little over a week ago to those two poor girls. Wren told me that they got the bear, but something about the whole situation still unsettles me.

I agree, trying not to overthink it. I haven't been out since I hurt my ankle, but I will take him on a shorter, more popular trail just to ease myself back into it. Plus, I don't think he has ever hiked in his life. I don't want to take him on a hard trail to start.

"Good. I'll pick you up after work."

"Do you mind if I bring my dog Moon?" I ask. "I haven't gotten her out in a while, and she would love it." Thinking about the attack, I note she will warn us if any animals get too close.

"Of course! Want me to pick her up before I get you?"

"If it's not too much trouble, that would be great! My parents will be off tomorrow so they can help you get her into your car."

"Sounds good. It'll be nice to see where you grew up."

Butterflies flutter in my stomach as he says that. I'm sure my house is much different than where he grew up.

With one final kiss to the cheek, I head out to my car.

At home, I'm exhausted from not getting much sleep last night. I get my pajamas on and climb into bed.

As my head connects with my pillow, I already feel myself drifting off, but before I enter the blackness, one thought travels through my head.

I haven't heard one word from Wren since I left. No calls. No texts. Nothing.

The coffee shop is crazy busy the next morning, leaving me no time to overthink hiking with Liam. Or Wren's silence. Liam seems more like the guy you would find on a golf course, not in the forest, but we shall see how it goes.

I'm also very surprised to not hear one word about the

attack. Everyone is acting like it never happened.

After changing into hiking clothes and grabbing the backpack I left in my car, I lean against the hood and wait for Liam.

Within a minute, he pulls up and the sight makes me laugh.

He's driving a black BMW convertible. Moon is sitting in the front seat, one paw up on the door, looking very proud of herself.

Liam shoots me a killer smile and steps out of the car to open my door. I push Moon into the back seat, earning myself a glare from the dog, like how could I possibly make her sit in the back?

Liam closes my door then walks around to the driver's side. I notice that he has traded the slacks for athletic shorts, and can't help admiring the tight fabric accentuating his butt as he walks in front of the car. "All right, where are we going?"

I'm about to direct him out of the parking lot when I look to my right and see Wren standing at the edge of the trees, staring at me. Why is he here?

My blood instantly begins to stir, and the desire returns.

What is wrong with me?

———

I choose a trail that is an easy three mile round-trip and ends at a beautiful lake.

Moon pulls at the leash as I clip it to her collar. "I know

baby, but you need to wear this on this trail," I tell her in a soothing voice. "There are too many people for you to run free."

When I straighten, Liam is looking at me. "How come I never knew you had a dog? You two seem very close."

I scratch Moon's ears. "She was just another part of home that I tried to forget."

Liam puts his own backpack on, and I give him a point for being prepared. Maybe I am not giving him enough credit. He is in good shape; this probably isn't his first hike.

As we start to walk, Liam asks, "Why were you trying to forget this place? It's absolutely beautiful. I think I have fallen in love even in the short time I have been here."

That's not a simple question and I don't know how much I want to share with Liam. One of the reasons I like being around him is because he doesn't know my past. He didn't know me when I was in diapers, like most people in town.

"I just felt like I needed to branch out and see the world, or at least more than my small town. I did, and now I know this is where I want to be."

We start walking up a steeper hill and I'm impressed that Liam holds pace with me. With Moon pulling on the leash, we're moving quickly.

"I can understand that. With my dad owning and running his company, I was expected to follow in his footsteps. I felt very much like my path was already paved for me, even before I was born. Amtika is successful now, but it was a big shock when I branched out and started it. At first, it didn't look like it would succeed, but I just started working harder.

"Sometimes family doesn't realize they are suffocating you when they are just trying to help."

Wow. I didn't think he would understand, but he does. This is my life and I am not going to let anything dictate how I live it. This makes me think about Wren and the intense connection I have with him, as if something more is pushing me in his direction.

As the lake comes into view, all my other thoughts become clear as I take in the beauty. The turquoise water is surrounded by high mountain peaks. At a few hundred feet wide, the lake dominates the landscape. I scan to the island in the middle and remember swimming to it once as a teenager. It was one of the many shenanigans Mark, Tollen, and I had gotten into growing up. Not something I ever plan on doing again. With the water barely above freezing, we had to run back to the car to stay warm after we got back to shore.

I take a seat on a large rock where I motion for Liam to join me. We'd carried a steady conversation on the hike up but now we sit in silence, listening to the peaceful sounds of nature.

Moon whines, wanting to explore. Since we're alone, I let her off the leash. She bounds down into the water, unbothered by the chill. She wades in and dips her head, enjoying the feeling of the cool water on her face.

Liam grabs my hand. "This is really nice. Thank you for

giving me a second chance. I know I've messed up more than once."

He is right. This is nice. I don't know where it is going, but Liam seems to want to take it slow as well.

Suddenly, the hair on my back of my neck prickles. I get the distinct feeling I am being watched. I scan our surroundings. No one is there. I look at Moon. Her ears are perked, and she's sniffing the air. She feels it, too. I didn't imagine it.

I scan the edge of the forest for the source of my unease. That's when I see it. Two yellow eyes stare back at me from the thickest part of the forest. The wolf.

What is he doing here? We are miles away from the last place I saw him. Is he following me? Protecting me?

I never told my father that I saw a wolf. Maybe it was because I thought I'd imagined it. I haven't heard any recent rumors about wolf sightings.

When I blink and look back, he is gone. *Did* I imagine it again? Am I going crazy?

I shiver. "We should head back."

I leave Moon off the leash hoping she will warn us if there is something around.

I keep my senses on high alert as we walk back down the trail. Since I don't say a word, Liam can probably tell I am tense, but doesn't ask what's wrong until we're back in the car. "Was it something I said?"

"No. Nothing. I thought I might have seen something in the forest when we were sitting by the lake. That's all. But I probably imagined it."

Liam's eyes widen. "Something, like a bear?" He is such a city boy; it's kind of cute.

"Yeah, something like that. Moon never barked, so I might have just been seeing things, but I was trying to be cautious. I didn't want to freak you out."

"I heard there was a bear attack that killed two girls here." I nod.

Liam doesn't head back to the shop, where my car is parked. "Where are you going? My car is the other way. I should have been giving you directions, but I thought you'd learned your way around pretty well."

"I know where I am going. This is the way to your house. When I was there earlier, your mom invited me over for dinner. We can get your car later."

Liam. At my house. For dinner.

I never worried with Mark because he's known me forever and Wren already knew my dad. But Liam is different. He has gotten a glimpse into my life here, but it is so different than the one I lived when I was in the city. This will be a good test to see if he truly has changed. I love my parents, but they can be a little out there. I loved my life growing up, but it was very different from most people's childhoods.

I still don't know what caused Liam's mind to change. He seemed very done and then all of a sudden, he is here doing everything I want trying to get me back. I shouldn't forgive him. But I have enjoyed our time together. Why does my brain seem to stop functioning when it comes to guys?

We pull up to my house, and the moment I open the car door, Moon barrels out, heading to the kitchen to see what my mom is cooking and if there are any scraps to spare.

As we walk up to the door, my dad greets us at the front porch while sizing up Liam and his car. After introductions, my dad takes Liam to show him the house and most likely to try to strike the fear of God into him if he hurts his baby girl.

All the other boys I have brought home have been boys my parents already knew. Liam is new and I can feel suspicion coming from my dad.

I find my mom in the kitchen making manicotti, one of my favorite foods, and sneaking a piece of cheese to Moon. "How was your hike?"

"Great! Liam did better than I expected. I didn't think he was what you would call an outdoorsy guy."

"He seems polite enough, but his car gives him away." She chuckles because we both know that that car would not work well up here once winter comes.

"Yeah, he came up for a few days to say hi. He's probably heading back soon. I don't really know his plans. We didn't talk about it."

My mom gives me a curious look and then says, "I was waiting for you to explain but you don't appear to be spilling the beans on your own, so I'll just ask. Who is he? It's not every day we get a polished man driving a convertible saying he is here to pick up Moon to go on a hike with you." My mom tries to keep it light, but I hear some tension in her voice. Did he do something that made her not like him?

I haven't told my mom about what happened with Liam. Who would? There are some things you just don't want to share with your mother.

"He is a friend from when I worked at Amtika."

"Just a friend? How come you never mentioned him? You know you can talk to me, Jamie. I'm here to listen and help. I have made a lot of mistakes myself over the years, and they have made me wiser."

Just as I am about to spill everything, Liam and my father walk in. Liam gives me a smile as he sees my worried face. You never quite know what you are going to get with my father.

Mom announces that dinner is ready and we all head into the dining room. It feels strange to be eating in here. Normally, we only use this table for special occasions or holidays. I'm happy my parents are being extra polite with Liam; I'm still waiting for something crazy to happen and for him to run for the hills. So far so good, but we still have dinner to get through.

As we all sit down my mom opens a bottle of wine and says to Liam, "Thank you for bringing the wine. I figured tonight is as good as any to drink it."

When did Liam do that? He is totally trying to suck up to my parents.

During dinner, the conversation stays light, and we end up finishing the bottle. Just as I'm about to get up and help clear the dishes, Moon yips from the living room, alerting us that someone is at the front door.

As I carry the dishes to the kitchen, my dad answers the door. Liam offers to help in the kitchen, and I give him a look and ask playfully, "Have you ever done dishes before?"

He answers with a laugh. "Yes, Jamie, I know how to do dishes. Do I routinely do them? No. But they are much more enjoyable when they are being done next to a gorgeous woman."

Blushing from his comment, I tear away from his intense stare to see who was at the door. I peer beyond my father's body and stop when I see Wren.

If looks could kill, Liam wouldn't be alive any longer. Wren is angry, the fury practically burning behind his eyes.

But he doesn't do anything. He just turns back to my father and says, "The sheriff just informed me that we have a missing family on the northeastern side of the park. It was reported an hour ago when they hadn't returned to their hotel to meet up with the other family they traveled here with. Their car has been located at the Bear Creek trailhead, but there is no sight of them."

For the next few minutes, they exchange conversation as I listen, going over various logistics.

"The sheriff has already gathered a team of his men, but there are children involved and he wants to get on this quickly. Everyone's a little on edge since the bear attack."

Before I can think, my voice says, "I can help."

My dad turns towards me. I know he is going to tell me why it is a bad idea for me to go, but before he has the chance, Wren jumps in.

"John, she can stay with me and I can keep an eye on her. We need all the eyes we can get if we want to find them tonight."

Great. I need to stay away from him. I can't seem to control my feelings when he is near. But it is too late now, so I say, "Let me change. I'll be down in five and ready to go."

Liam's eyes are on me as I head to my bedroom. Before I can get there, he calls to me. I try to ignore him because I know what he's going to say, but when I reach my bedroom, he reaches it at the same time and steps in with me. "Are you sure you know what you're doing?"

I give him a look. *I am changing. What are you doing in here?*

Understanding, he replies, "Jamie, I have seen you naked hundreds of times. I am a grown man; I can control myself around a beautiful naked woman."

Not wanting to waste time, I go into my closet and pull out jeans, a thermal top, and my hiking boots, then strip and dress quickly.

When I am finished, Liam steps closer, so that his nose is touching mine. "I had other ideas of how tonight would end. Are you sure you don't want to make an excuse and come back with me?"

I take a step back. "I need to help. These woods are dangerous at night and an inexperienced family will not fare well. Plus, I thought we agreed to take this slow. It's been two days."

He brushes a piece of hair out of my face. "Please be careful out there and text me when you get back. I will be worrying until I hear from you. If I didn't think I would be more of a burden than a help, I would volunteer, too."

With that, we head downstairs. Wren and my father are still discussing the matter, circling areas on a map. As I head toward them, Liam grabs my arm and pulls me back, placing a light kiss on my lips.

He steps back and walks towards the door, "Jamie, be careful and text me. I will be in town a few more days so let's make plans."

Before I can respond, he leaves.

I turn towards my father and Wren. My father seems unfazed, but Wren looks as if his skin is rippling, as if he might explode in anger. He says, "Excuse me," and quickly walks toward the back door.

That was weird.

I peer over my father's shoulder to see what they have worked up while I was upstairs changing. The map has several areas circled and numbered.

As I'm studying it, trying to get my bearings, my dad murmurs, "I think Wren has feelings for you. He typically is a very calm guy, but he always seems to get riled up around you."

I simply nod because the last thing I want to do is talk

about boys with my father. "I'm going to see if Wren is ready to go. It's been dark for an hour and we need to start looking."

Outside, Wren is pacing. When he sees me, he stops and gives me an accusing stare. Without saying another word, he walks back in the house, brushing against me as he passes. There is a quick shock as his arm touches mine, and then he is gone.

I return to the living room a few seconds later to find my father standing there, alone.

"Wren said to meet him in his car whenever you are ready."

I nod.

Just before I reach the door, my dad's voice calls out, "Please be careful Jamie. Your mom and I are still freaked out about the last incident. Just don't lose track of Wren and you will be fine."

I respond, "I will, Dad. You take care of yourself, too."

With that, I walk out the door.

I imagine spending the night with Wren, walking around the forest. This could turn into a very interesting night.

Chapter 19:

The drive is full of awkward silence. Neither of us have anything to say. I just sit there and look out the window.

What happened at that party long ago is the source of all my problems. If it hadn't happened, I'd probably be living happily ever after with Mark. I have been confused and mad at myself for so long because of that one night. I never would have done that to Mark if I could have helped it.

There is just something about Wren that makes my brain stop functioning. The desire that sparks when I am near him doesn't seem real. It's like a spell or a curse.

I'm on the edge of my seat, as far away from Wren as possible. There is a heat radiating from him, and I keep thinking about the sparks of electricity I feel whenever he touches me, even in the most innocent way.

It's only been a few days since the night we spent together at his house. I felt so wanted. But he betrayed me, fucked me, then left. Not to mention that he hasn't spoken to me since that night. He's not much better than Liam, and seems in it for the sex.

What feels like forever later, we arrive at the trailhead. There are multiple cars and about thirty people milling around.

As we get out of the car, I see Mark amidst the chaos and walk over to him. He asks, "What are you doing here?"

I give him a quick hug then explain. "Wren stopped by my house to tell my dad, and I volunteered to help. Any extra set of eyes is going to be helpful."

Still looking concerned, he reaches into his cruiser and hands me a radio and a container of bear spray. "Keep these with you just in case. Jamie, don't be a hero and stay safe."

With those words, he walks away to help another group.

Wren appears at my side. I didn't notice him until he was standing right next to me. He isn't touching me, but I kind of wish he was.

Jamie, stop it! You are here to help the family. You can put your problems away until they are found.

Wren says his first words since we left my house. "We will be taking quadrant four. It runs along the creek so it will be a little rough, but I figure you can handle it. I already checked in, so we are good to get started. Don't lose sight of me and tell me if my pace is too fast."

I would rather chop my own foot off than admit I can't keep up. Adjusting the radio and clutching the bear spray, I follow Wren as he sets off at a blistering pace.

As we enter the forest, a thought crosses my mind: I wonder if bear spray works on wolves.

I quickly find myself out of breath as I try to keep up with Wren. We aren't on a path and the ground is rough. The headlamp I'm wearing adds some light, but it's still difficult to see all of the obstacles.

By the third time I stumble, Wren turns around and looks at me. "Need me to slow down?"

"No, I'm fine. I can handle it." *I can handle you.*

He slows his pace slightly. My legs are grateful, but I feel like he's won by doing it.

The slower pace gives my mind a chance to wander. Wren hasn't mentioned the other night once and has been keeping the conversation to an absolute minimum. I know he's pissed about me and Liam, but does he forget? *I* was pissed first.

After another hour of silence, I can't stand it any longer. I explode. "Why didn't you tell me? That night plagued me for years, it still does, and you knew it was me the whole time!"

Wren flips around so fast I run into his chest. I try to move away but he puts his arms around me, holding me in place.

"I did tell you. You didn't want to listen."

Distracted by his body pressed against mine, it takes effort to get the next words out. "What gives you the right to treat me that way?"

"I have the right to do whatever I want. You belong to me. You always have."

Belong to him? What the fuck is he talking about? I don't belong to anyone. This isn't the eighteen-hundreds!

Just as I am about to tell him to shove it where the sun doesn't shine, his mouth comes crashing down on mine. His lips send sparks through my body, igniting the passion I have been shoving down.

I feel us moving until my back connects with a tree. The rough bark scrapes my back as Wren devours my mouth. Everything feels right when we are together.

I snake my hands under his shirt and feel his warm skin. My fingers tingle with pleasure as I run them over his chest. My mouth greedily takes as much as it is given. I tease at the hem of his pants.

Any rational thought is lost. I need him. Now.

He pulls away slightly and says, "I was so mad earlier when I saw that guy kiss you. You. Are. Mine."

His? Do I want to be his? Would it be so bad to be his?

A growl comes from his throat as his mouth returns to mine. There is a new intensity and I feel his hand move under my shirt. Stroking, feeling, claiming every inch of me as his.

His hands are on my pants' button, unhooking it and pulling the zipper down. As his hand finds its target, I moan into his mouth. My desire builds quickly as his hand claims me.

I feel myself explode, biting down on his lip until I taste blood. He leans back with a smile as he licks the blood away.

Destiny

He moves to unbutton his pants as I reach to pull mine down.

A blood curdling scream pierces the air, making us both stop.

We quickly right ourselves and race in the direction the scream came from. Wren is quicker than me and I lose him. I continue to head in the direction I think the scream came from but quickly become disoriented. Everything is so dark. My brain flashes back to the night I was stumbling around the woods, alone.

I have never feared the dark, but, suddenly, terror coils in my stomach. Off to my left, a loud howl echoes through the air. I don't want to yell for Wren and attract something else, so I quickly move away from the sound.

I use the headlamp to lighten the forest floor to keep from tripping. After a hundred feet, I come across a jacket laying on the ground. I lean down to pick it up and recoil quickly.

It is covered in blood.

My heart beats faster. I reach for the radio, but as I am pulling it out of my backpack, it slips out of my hand.

I stand up and scan the ground, trying to locate where it fell, and I'm stopped in my tracks by what I see. The family. Or what is left of them.

A mangled pile of flesh and clothing, lying no more than ten feet away. There is blood everywhere.

My stomach lurches at the sight. We are too late.

And now I am standing alone. At night. In the middle of the forest. Near a fresh kill. Even if the animal that did it isn't still around, it will attract everything that smells it.

Chapter 20:

Miraculously, I fan my hands out and locate the radio. I pick it up and push the button. "Anyone there?"

There is a pause, not more than a few seconds, but it feels like an eternity before I receive a response. "Copy, can I ask who this is and your location?" The voice cuts through the silent night air and I cringe, hoping that it isn't going to attract anything.

Jamie calm down, there is a lot of back up nearby and you just have to inform them where you are. "This is Jamie, Wren and I are in quadrant four. I have been temporarily separated from him, but I have found the family."

"Okay, Jamie, I need you to take a deep breath and stay calm. Do you think you could give me a general idea of where you are? Wren has a GPS monitor on him, but you said you got separated?"

I answer quickly, trying to give the best directions I can to my location. He tells me to just sit tight and help will arrive soon.

Not something I like to admit often, but I'm scared. I hope they arrive before whatever attacked these people decides to come back.

Bear spray in one hand and the radio in the other, I lean with my back against a tree, about twenty feet away from the mangled family, and wait.

I don't know where Wren is or who the scream came from. There is so much blood, it is hard to see if it's the whole family or someone was able to get away. I hope they did.

A branch breaks and I look up. I stay quiet so whatever is near won't see me.

Green eyes stare back at me. As my headlamp shines on them, they glow, and I realize what they belong to. A wolf.

Not the black wolf I've seen before. This one is different, smaller, with a reddish-grey coat. He studies me, not as prey, but with an almost human expression of confusion. Without a sound, the wolf lies down and continues to watch me.

For the first time, I'm not scared. I don't know why, but I know he wasn't the one to kill the family. He doesn't seem to be interested in the dead bodies, only me. Something about him looks familiar. I study him as he begins to lick one of his paws. Why does he look familiar? I have only seen one other wolf in my life, the black wolf, but they don't look anything alike.

His eyes. I know those eyes. How do I know those eyes?

As I'm racking my brain, trying to make the connection,

Destiny

footsteps come pounding through the forest. Part of me panics. He needs to leave. If anyone else sees him, they might shoot him!

As I get to my feet, expecting the search party, Wren comes into sight, carrying a young girl in his arms.

I don't know how to explain what happens next. He walks right up to the wolf. The wolf and Wren look at each other like they are communicating and then the wolf rubs his body along Wren's and takes off.

As I watch him disappear into the forest, it hits me where I recognize those eyes from. They look like my father's, like my brother's.

Wren says, "Backup will be here soon. They were able to pinpoint my location after you talked with them."

He sets the little girl down in my lap. She is wearing his coat, and her chest is moving. She is alive but unconscious. There is blood on her shirt, but I can't tell if it is hers or one of her family members.

Wren leaves her with me and heads over to the other family members.

I am glad that he is here, but how did he know where I was? He just showed up out of nowhere. He must've been nearby and heard me talking on the radio.

Wren speaks into the radio, "We have one young girl here who has been scratched. Do you have an ETA?"

I drown out the rest of the conversation. This girl in my arms is an orphan. She has lost her whole family.

Wanting to help in some way, I look the girl over for injuries. I'm sure Wren has already done this, and I'm not a doctor, so I don't really know what I am looking for.

I notice blood on the front of her shirt and locate a scratch on her lower abdomen. It's not very deep but it looks irritated. The skin surrounding it is puffy and red, on the verge of being infected.

Wren walks back over to sit down next to me. He puts his hand on my shoulder and asks, "Are you okay? I should have gone slower and made sure you stayed with me."

I can't help but become defensive. "I can take care of myself."

"I know you can, but I was worried when you weren't behind me. Whether you like it or not, I care about you."

Before I can reply, someone shouts Wren's name. Wren yells back, alerting the rest of the rescue party to our location.

As soon as they arrive, things happen quickly. Orders are given, areas taped off, and the mood turns from frantic to somber. This was almost the worst outcome that could have occurred. The only bright spot is the little girl, though it's heartbreaking to know what she's lost.

I am still holding her in my arms, far away from the crews who are inspecting the scene, when her temperature starts to spike. She still hasn't woken up. I shine my headlight at the scratch and it looks even more inflamed than last time I checked.

Just as I am about to try to get someone's attention, Wren

walks over. "It's been decided that I will take her to The Academy."

What? The Academy? Why?

As he sweeps her up into his arms, I jump up and follow him. "Wren, I think she has an infection. We need to take her to the hospital."

He doesn't break his pace. "Jamie, the hospital won't be able to help her."

I lose step with him and wind up staring after him, confused. What's that supposed to mean?

So many times, when Wren is talking, I feel like I am missing half the knowledge I need to understand him. This is part of his job, so he knows better than me what this girl needs.

I catch up with him. Fairly quickly, we find the trail and get back to the parking lot.

I follow Wren to his silver Jeep Wrangler, where he places the girl in the back seat.

She doesn't look good and I don't understand why he's not more freaked out about her state. Shouldn't we be rushing her to the hospital?

Wren motions for me to get in the Jeep, but I stand my ground. "Don't you think we should—"

"God dammit, Jamie, just get in the Jeep."

Crossing my arms over my chest I look him straight in the eye and say, "No."

He steps closer to me and says, "Why are you fighting this

so hard? You belong with me Jamie, don't you feel it?"

Standing my ground, I say, "I belong to me, Wren, not anybody else." As I turn to walk away, I say, "I hope you get home safely."

He gets in his Jeep and slams the door. Then he peels out of the parking lot. Serves him right for acting that way. Who does he think he is, always trying to tell me what to do?

But I hope that girl is okay. The Academy? What is he expecting they'll do?

After the anger dies down, I look around, realizing I am going to need to find another ride home. I spot Mark among a group of other officers.

When he sees me, he pulls me into a tight hug. "Are you okay? I heard you found the bodies."

All the emotions of the night well up. Wren's hot and cold attitude, how terrified I was in the forest when the wolf howled, finding the dismembered family. The tears come hot and heavy and I soon soak Mark's shirt. He slowly rubs my back, telling me it is going to be okay.

Once I've calmed down, he holds me out in front of him and gives me a once-over. "Why don't you get in the car and I will drive you home? There isn't much else for me to do here."

I only do it because he asked; he didn't demand, like Wren. A few minutes later, I'm in his patrol car, heading home.

Mark puts his hand on my leg. I don't think he's trying to make a move, it's just to comfort me. I drift off and wake up when Mark is opening the car door outside my house.

He helps me up to the door. "Please call me if you need anything. I remember the first time I was exposed to something like that. It's heavy. I almost threw up."

I hug him and say, "Thanks, Mark."

Just as I am opening the door, he says, "We never got a chance to have that dinner you mentioned. Are you free Wednesday? My treat."

Too tired to think, I nod at him and wave goodbye.

I fall into bed, entering sleep almost immediately.

I dream of a dark forest and green-eyed wolves.

Chapter 21:

I wake up to two text messages, but neither is the one I was hoping to get. As much as I want to stay away from Wren, I also want him to care. Our relationship has been so explosive. Sometimes he seems like he cares, yet other times I get the feeling he wishes he never met me.

I fall back into bed and pull the pillow over my eyes. I feel like I am in high school with this drama. The back and forth is killing me. We are adults, why can't we just handle this situation as mature individuals?

Like Liam. He has been nothing but polite and open with me.

The first text is from him. He had an emergency and had to head back to the city. He said he would call when he gets the chance. I don't know why he is acting so stable and together. Part of me thinks it's all an act.

And then there is sweet and kind Mark. His text is to check in and make sure I'm all right after last night. It was a big night, but I feel surprisingly well, considering. I am worried about the little girl, though. She seemed so defenseless. She must be scared to death.

Knowing I need to get out of bed, I swing my feet over the side and head toward the bathroom.

Hopefully my dad is home so I can get some more information about the little girl.

As I enter the kitchen, my dad is sitting at the center island, drinking coffee. He looks tired. I wonder when he got home last night and if he has slept at all.

He stands up and pulls me into a hug. "When I heard you had gotten separated from Wren and found the remains of the family last night, I almost had a heart attack. I'm not sure I want you out on any more search and rescues. Something weird is going on. I think it best to stay out of the forest for the moment. That means no hiking."

At least I wasn't the only one to find the recent events strange. I wonder again if it is related to the wolves. I've seen two of them, yet nobody else has mentioned them. I never felt any threat from either of them. If anything, I felt like they were protecting me. I don't want anything to hurt them, which is what I tell myself when I again decide not to mention them to my father.

Still hugging my dad, I think back to last night. What would have done that to that poor family? They didn't look like they had been eaten, just attacked. Animals don't just do that without a reason.

Pulling back so that I can see my dad's face, I ask, "Do you or any of the guys have any idea what did this? Do they think it's related to the two girls that were killed a few weeks ago?"

I know Wren said he got the bear that killed those girls, but how would he know if it was the right bear?

My dad grabs me some coffee before returning to sit next to me at the breakfast bar. "Honestly Jamie, the only time I have ever seen anything like this was when your brother and his friends were attacked. I still think about it every day and how we never found out what attacked them."

My heart hurts at the mention of my brother. It wasn't like we never talked about him, but it wasn't a common conversation topic. We all missed him and didn't feel the need to bring up the horrible way he died.

Taking a much-needed drink of my coffee, I say, "I wasn't very old when Jacob died, but I do remember the way everyone acted. It was like everyone was trying to figure out what happened, and then one day people just lost interest. It was strange. Maybe this time we will figure out what actually happened to this poor family. How is the little girl?"

He shakes his head. "She died. Last night."

I gasp. "But— Wren said he was taking her to--"

"He knew someone who he thought could help. But she died before he could get her there."

I clamp a hand over my heart. That poor little girl.

My dad looks sad as he responds, "For now, I need you

to stay out of the forest. We have no idea what is causing this, and I need to know you are safe."

I take his hand in mine to comfort him. He is normally so strong and determined. It is hard to see my father this beaten down. "Don't worry, Dad, I'll stay out of the forest, but you need to promise me you will be careful, too."

He smiles sadly. "It's a promise."

Last night after dinner, I sat in the kitchen with my parents and played cards for hours, just like old times. Some families like board games, but we were always card people. My brother taught me how to play blackjack when I was six years old. He always thought I was cheating because I would win so much. He always joked with my dad that they needed to take me to the casinos when I turned twenty-one.

I walk up the trail next to the creek for my shift at the coffee shop. It's been two days, but the town is still buzzing about what happened to the family last weekend. The official word is that it was a bear attack. The locals seem to be staying away from the forest now, but it is peak tourist season. The rangers have posted warnings, but my father says tourists aren't taking them very seriously.

I hope nobody else gets hurt, but after everything that's happened, I fear it is inevitable.

I still haven't heard from Wren. I feel like half of my time is spent waiting to see if he will contact me. With the way he left it, I will not be reaching out to him, but I want to know what happened that night with the little girl. Nobody has really mentioned that she was found alive, which I find strange. The newspapers simply say that the whole family was killed.

Liam has been freaking out since he heard what happened and keeps asking me to come stay with him in the city. I've already run away once, and I don't plan on doing it again. He sends me a text every hour, checking on me. Generally I would find it annoying, but with Wren giving me radio silence, it is nice to know someone cares.

The area is deserted as I pull out the key and go to unlock the shop's front door. It's early—the sun hasn't even popped up over the mountains yet—but I have to get ready before my shift. I've never felt uncomfortable opening the shop before, but this morning, something tickles the back of my neck. I can't shake the feeling like something is watching, so as I scrabble to force the key into the lock, I keep scanning the forest around me.

As I get the door open, there's the unmistakable sound of a cracking branch behind me. I spin quickly, and can swear I see a flash of black disappearing into the forest, making me think of the wolf with the yellow eyes. I hustle inside and close the door, sweating and breathing heavy. Maybe finding the family is affecting me more than I thought, like Mark said. I'm having dinner with him tonight, so I'll talk with him about it.

Finally catching my breath, I rush behind the counter to

prepare for the day. I turn the music up loud, hoping to drain out my thoughts and calm my nerves.

Suddenly, a hand falls on my shoulder. I jump and whirl around, tossing the bag of coffee beans in my hands into the air. As beans fly all over the room, I realize it's just Roberta.

"Shit! Roberta, you scared me! I didn't hear you come in."

"I'm surprised you can hear anything with the music this loud. Everything all right?"

She must be able to feel my tension. The whole town is on edge after what happened. She looks at the clock and motions me to the couch. "Let's sit down for a minute. Tell me what is bothering you."

I nod because I need to get my head on straight before I start serving people.

I tell Roberta about this weekend and finding the family. I even mention the wolves, which I haven't done to anyone else. There is something about Roberta that makes me trust her and I know she won't think I am crazy or tell anyone else.

She lets me finish then puts her hand on my knee. "Awful. Sounds like you had a rough couple of days. Do you want to go home and let me take over?"

I shake my head because the last thing I need is more time by myself to overthink everything.

"Are you sure? Well, I was planning on doing inventory so I will be around if you need me. And I wouldn't worry about the wolves. It sounds like they have chosen you and are protecting you. I would go with your gut instinct with them."

Chosen me? Something about the way she says it makes me think she knows more and isn't telling me.

"I feel like you know everything about me, Roberta, like *seriously*, everything. But I know so little about you. I'll respect it if you don't want to tell me, but I feel bad that our conversations are always so one sided."

Roberta smiles. "I'm an open book. I was just waiting for you to ask. It's about time!"

She is such an interesting old lady. I love how quirky she is.

My inquiry opens the floodgates. We both stand up and begin to clean up the beans I spilled everywhere as she tells me her story.

"When I was twelve years old, my family moved here. We came to town so my brother could attend The Academy. I wasn't allowed to in those days because I was a girl, so I went to the small school we had in town."

As we continue to get ready for customers, Roberta tells me her life story, and what a life story it is. She has outlived two husbands and used the money that was left to her by her second husband to transform this building into the coffee shop twenty years ago. Before that, she worked at The Academy for many years.

I ask her for her secret to having so much energy and she starts talking about herbs and crystals, losing me quickly. I have always been interested in science and don't believe any of the spiritual energy stuff, but if it works for her, I am happy.

The day flies by and soon it is time to head home. I give Roberta a hug before I leave, feeling more connected to her than ever before.

As I walk out the door, I pull out my phone. I have texts from Liam and Mark but still nothing from Wren. I break and decide to send him a quick text.

Jamie: What happened with the girl?

The three little dots appear almost instantly and then his response comes through.

Wren: She died.

So wordy, that Wren. *And?* I type in.

No response.

After that, I send ten more texts to Wren, but I don't receive any reply.

Chapter 22:

Mark picks me up precisely at six that evening. He looks nice in khaki pants and a button-down shirt, and I can tell he took extra time getting dressed. As I get into his car, I have major déjà vu. All the times I did this in high school come flooding back.

I smile at Mark, not wanting to bring up the past. Even so, there's a steady flow of easy conversation as soon as I get in the car that continues through dinner. We decide to go to the same Italian place I went with Tollen since we both like it.

Since I haven't had the time to really catch up with Mark, it's nice to hear how everything went for him over the past few years. As we are finishing up dessert, I finally bring up the family that was attacked and how nervous I've been. A shadow crosses Mark's face. "Yeah. It's crazy. The whole incident is. Two incidents like that, so close together ... what does your father say?"

"He's worried. We all are."

As we walk out to the car, the mood has dampened with talk of the incident. It's early, so I ask if he wants to go back to my parents' house and watch a movie.

"What about my place?" he says.

I haven't seen his place yet. I can tell he doesn't want to be presumptive, but we are adults now.

We drive across town to his apartment. As we walk up the stairs, he seems quiet. I'm not sure if he is nervous about me being here or is still upset about the incident that happened this past weekend. We were having such a good time; I don't know why I had to bring it up.

He opens the door to his second story apartment and I look around. It is good-sized, fairly up-to-date, and neat for a bachelor pad. It reminds me a little of the apartment I had when I lived in the city, but with a much better view.

Mark gives me a quick tour; the rooms are clean but not spotless, which makes me smile. Liam's apartment always felt fake because he had someone clean every day. This feels lived-in, like a home, and it makes me smile when I see Toby's room. It looks as if a pink bomb has exploded.

Mark hears me laugh and asks what's up.

"You used to hate all the girly stuff. You would never even hold my purse, but now look at you. Father to a little girl and she looks like she gets everything her heart desires."

He smiles. "I never thought I would want a little girl until I had one. She is so perfect; I couldn't even imagine not having her in my life now. I may go a little overboard, but I feel bad that she gets moved back and forth, so I want her to have everything she needs when she comes here."

I place my hand on his arm. "You are a great father. She adores you."

He smiles, and I catch him looking at my hand on his arm. It's not an invitation. I quickly take it away.

"Do you have anything in mind to watch or should I start looking?" I head over to the couch and grab the remote.

Mark hesitates for a second before coming over. He sits on the other side of the couch, away from me. "Whatever you want."

As I turn on the TV and flip through channels, it hits me. This is the first time we've been alone, in private, since I left him.

I have been putting it off, but we need to talk about us. Or the lack of an *us*.

"Mark." I say his name so he will look over at me. "Um … well … I don't really know how to start …"

He cuts me off and says, "I love Tollen." I freeze, not expecting those words. "I wouldn't take back what we had, but I have moved on. I have been wanting to talk to you but there has never been a good time."

This is what I want, so why do I feel a little hurt? They deserve to be happy. Mark was mine, but he isn't anymore.

"I wanted to tell you right away, but Tollen wanted me to hold off. You didn't handle the Toby situation well, so she wanted to wait. We are kind of dating, but Tollen is worried what you will think so we've kept it quiet."

He pauses, waiting for a response. I need to respond. "Mark, I'm super happy for you. I was actually going to suggest you guys try dating. I feel dumb for not catching on sooner."

I can tell Mark is nervous and he lets out a large breath at my words. "You're not dumb, Jamie. It's all very new. I knew I had feelings for her, but it took seeing you again for me to act on them."

I smile at him. My best friends have found their way to each other.

"Jamie, could I ask you a favor? Tollen feels guilty about the whole thing. Could you talk to her?"

"Of course, Mark."

My best friends together and happy is the best thing that has happened since I returned home.

Chapter 23:

Finally in a rhythm, the next week flies by. Liam is still tied up in the city but promises he will be up tomorrow to take me to dinner and will be staying through the weekend. The coffee shop is running smoothly, and I've convinced Roberta to order some more New Adult books since we have such a young crowd that frequents the shop.

Making coffee while talking to people in town has been nice, but getting more involved with the business side and book purchasing is my favorite part of the job. All my life, I'd wanted to join a big company and climb the ladder. It was stable, consistent, and predictable. But now I am seeing a lot of positives to owning a small business, being involved in every decision, and working toward its success.

I don't even want to think about Wren, but I can't help it. We haven't talked or texted since he told me the girl had died. I haven't even seen him. Roberta tells me he comes in all the time, just not when I am around. What is he playing at?

I don't know why I care. Things with Liam are going well. We seem to be connecting on a much deeper level than before. We still haven't been intimate yet; maybe this weekend. I figure I will know when it's time.

At two, I pick up my bag and prepare to leave. Roberta asked me to stay a little later today because she needed to run some errands. She walks in the door and after a few pleasantries, I say goodbye.

Distracted by digging in my purse for my keys, I don't notice him until I practically run into his solid, warm chest. I stumble because of the unexpected obstacle and his arms come up to steady me.

I look up into those yellow brown eyes I love and the desire hits me like a punch in the stomach. For a few moments neither of us say anything, just stare into each other's eyes. Whatever is between us doesn't feel sane and that is half the reason I need to stay away. I hate being pushed in any direction, even if it is towards a guy I am attracted to.

Determined not to be the one to break the silence, I wait for Wren to say something. It takes a while, but he finally cracks and speaks first.

"Hey."

"Hey, yourself."

"What are you doing here?"

"I work here. What are you doing here?"

"You get off at noon, and I'm at the coffee shop for coffee."

"Roberta had stuff to do so I stayed late." Why am I explaining myself to him?

He makes a move to sidestep me. "Oh, well, I should probably get going."

I clamp a hand on his wrist, surprising him. I have questions, and now that I am standing right here with him, he is going to answer some of them. "Why won't you respond to my texts? What happened to the girl? Why is everyone saying she died with her parents in the forest?"

He looks around and pulls me off to the side of the trail, away from the other people that are walking by. "Jamie, no. You aren't ready to know everything yet."

I stare at him, confused. "If not now, when?"

In answer, he presses his lips to mine gently before pulling away and entering the coffee shop.

Stunned, I touch my mouth, still feeling the pressure of his lips on mine. Why does he always kiss me?

I slide behind the wheel of my car and stay there for the longest time, trying to process the last few seconds. His words reverberate in my head. *You aren't ready to know everything yet.* What is he talking about?

I'm dressed and ready when Liam pulls up.

He is always so put together. His clothes fit him perfectly and always compliment his looks. They show off his body that I know he works very diligently on with a trainer to keep in top form.

I smile as I walk out to his car. I opted for a dress because, knowing him, I figured we would be going somewhere nice for dinner. He gets out of the driver's seat and walks around to open my door. He has such good manners.

He kisses my cheek lightly then closes the door behind me. As he is walking around the car, I see Moon barrel out of the forest to run up and greet him. He obliges her and scratches her ears as she licks his arm. Something about seeing him with my dog makes my heart hurt. He really seems like a good guy. He may not have treated me the best before, but he is making up for it now.

As he gets in the car, he looks over at me and just smiles. Then he says, "You are extremely beautiful, Jamie. I know I talked to you every day, but I still missed you."

"I missed you, too." Did I miss him, or did I just say that because that was the first thing to come to mind? "Where are we going to dinner?"

"I did some research and there is a seafood and steak place on the east side of town that looked really good. I made a reservation, but we can go wherever you would like."

I reply, "That sounds great. How has work been? Did the emergency get smoothed out?"

I've broached his favorite subject, work. He starts going into all the details. Part of me misses the fast-paced lifestyle I had when I worked for Liam, but I know that would only be true for a few weeks. Grinding is fun for a little while, but it becomes exhausting fast.

I'm so busy thinking about my old life in Denver that I only catch about half of what Liam is saying to me. Something about one of the drugs they created having unusual side effects in one of the trials.

As we arrive at the restaurant, I am excited to have a nice dinner and good conversation with Liam.

Dinner is fantastic. I ordinarily stay away from seafood when I am not close to the ocean, but the scallops were amazing. Afterwards, Liam asks if I would be interested in going back to the hotel for a drink.

I agree, not ready to go home yet. I know his intention is to get me in his room for other activities, as his sexual appetite has always been large. He's being polite about it, but I can tell he's getting anxious. I haven't decided if I am ready yet. Something in the back of my brain tells me it isn't a good idea.

We sit in one of the lounge chairs watching the sun set behind the mountains. I sip my Cosmo as he takes a big gulp of his scotch on the rocks. There are only a few clouds in the sky, so the sun puts on a real show of bright pinks and oranges before it tucks itself behind the mountain. Seriously, nature is so incredible. When I lived in the city, a building blocked so much of the view, I rarely got a chance to catch the sun.

Liam says, "It's incredibly beautiful. I think I have fallen in love with the beauty of this town."

When I look over at him, he is staring right at me. *Whoa there, boy, slow down, slow way down.*

I finish the rest of my drink and ask, "Want to go watch a movie in your room? It's still early, but I don't feel like drinking anymore."

He smiles. "Yes, that sounds wonderful."

As we walk to the elevator, he holds my hand. It feels nice being with him this way, especially since, before, we didn't touch much in public and tried to stay under the radar.

As the elevator takes us up, I tell him I have never been past the lobby in this hotel and I am excited to see the rooms. We walk to the end of the hall and he opens the door. I step in and am shocked by its size. I know this must be the best room in the hotel. It is huge!

Awestruck, I take a moment to walk in and look around. The whole side of the wall is glass and I faintly see the mountains outlined with the light from the moon. The living area is dominated by three large brown leather couches circling a glass coffee table with flowers sitting in the middle. On the left wall, there is a large gas fireplace with a chair tucked between it and the windows. I think about how that would be the perfect place to snuggle in and read a book on a snowy day. Off to the left, I see a fancy drink cart fully stocked with ice and bowls with sliced fruit for drinks.

As I walk around, I see all the little details making the room feel welcoming and classy at the same time. I find a door and walk into a room that houses a huge king bed draped with a gold and red comforter. The TV hanging on the wall must be 100 inches. Off to my right is the bathroom that

I can see is lined with white marble. I traveled with Liam for trips a few times, but this room is much nicer then where we had stayed before. Not that they weren't nice, this room just has an extra level of luxury.

I feel Liam follow me into the bedroom, he hands me a glass and says, "Its sparkling water with lime, I can get you something else if you would like, but downstairs you mentioned you were done drinking for the night."

"Thank you, this is perfect, and this room is incredible."

"It is, isn't it? When I called to book the room I had last time, the room was full, so they upgraded me to the penthouse suite."

"Well, I love it!" I walk over and hop on the bed, getting settled in to watch a movie. Liam takes a moment just to look at me then walks over. He sets his drink down and takes mine out of my hand to place on the bedside table before he straddles me and cages me in with his arms.

His voice sounds huskier when he talks and I know he is turned on, "Jamie, I know we are taking this slow, but I have been dreaming about your lips for months. Can I kiss you?"

He has already kissed me since he came up to see me, but I can see from his eyes that he isn't thinking just a peck. He wants to kiss me, really kiss me.

I look at his lips, they are plump and just the way I remember them. My brain flashes to when Wren kissed me yesterday, but I squish it down and press my lips to Liam's. They are warm and I can taste the scotch he was drinking earlier as he deepens the kiss.

It's not the fire I experienced with Wren, but I feel something for Liam. I just must figure out if I feel enough.

Liam knows how to kiss. Using pressure but not too much, the occasional nip, and just enough tongue. I feel his hands start to roam, but he doesn't move to remove my clothes. I can feel his want pressing against me, but I know he is waiting for me to take it further.

Liking the feeling of kissing him, I let my hands roam as well. I feel his hard muscle under his shirt, the distinct ridges of his defined stomach. Part of me wants to take it further tonight but another knows I am not ready. I don't want to rush this. After a few more minutes of making out with Liam, I pull back and smile, "I forgot how good of a kisser you are."

He gives me a wink. "Do I need to remind you how good I am at...?" He says, as he makes a motion with his hips, thrusting the air.

I laugh. I know he wants more, but he is being playful with me. "How could I forget? Maybe soon I'll let you remind me, but for tonight I just want to snuggle and watch a movie."

I can see slight disappointment flash into his eyes, but it is gone quickly. "I'm up for whatever gets me more time with you." He is so sweet. I'm just not ready yet. The way he handled it almost made me want to change my mind, but I remind myself there is no rush.

I snuggle into his side as I pick a new comedy that I have been wanting to watch. He kisses the top of my head and one of his hands is drawing small circles on my back. This is so nice.

I start to imagine what it would be like to be in a real relationship with Liam as my eyes grow heavy and I drift off.

I'm back in the forest. The grey wolf is on one side of me and the black wolf is on the other. We walk together, as a unit. I know they are here to protect me, but I don't know what from.

The forest is calm and quiet. Too quiet. I realize that there is no sound. No insects, no birds, not even our footsteps as we walk on the pine needles and sticks covering the forest floor.

We are on a journey; I don't know what it is or where we are going, but they will be with me until the end.

I feel a hand shaking me awake and then lips press to my mouth gently. Confused from my dream, it takes me a moment to return to reality. Liam is standing next to me.

"Hey beautiful. You fell asleep. I hate to wake you, but it's getting late and I want to drive you home."

I'm so comfortable and I want to get back to dreaming so I can figure out what journey I am supposed to be on. "If it's okay with you, I'd like to stay."

He replies, "Of course it is, but I wanted to give you the option to head home."

He walks back around the bed and throws me one of his t-shirts. "You can wear this if you want to be more comfortable." I hesitate because I don't want him to take my staying the wrong way; I'm still not ready to have sex with him. He sees my hesitation and adds, "Don't worry, Jamie. As much as I would love to do more, I won't until you're ready. I can sleep next to you in a t-shirt and not jump you."

I turn around and stand up, shedding my dress and bra then slipping on his T-shirt. When I turn around, I find him standing there just in his boxers and I take in his chiseled body. He looks better than I remember.

Catching me staring, he asks, "Like what you see?"

Embarrassed, I turn away and quickly jump under the covers. I feel him snuggle up behind me, pulling me in tight. His desire pushes into my back, but he does nothing about it.

I can't blame him; I am turned on, too. Feeling comfortable and safe, I drift off to sleep quickly. My dream doesn't return, but I get a lingering feeling that it was a warning.

Chapter 24:

I wake up the next morning with sun streaming in on my face. The blinds have been opened and a stunning view of the mountains looks back at me. I smile. This is really nice.

I look over. The bed is empty and the alarm clock says it's almost nine. I've never sleep this late. Must have been the bed. I don't know if I have ever slept in something so comfortable.

I shift to a sitting position and just take in the moment. This is everything I've always wanted with Liam, and now I have it. He didn't pressure me last night and I think my earlier hesitation at his intentions has passed. What we have now is so different than what we had before. I feel connected to him and he seems to care for me. Before, I could never tell if I was just convenient or if he was actually interested in me. I'm still curious what caused this change.

The smell of food and coffee drifts from the other room. As I am moving the covers back to get out of bed, Liam walks through the door.

He is wearing jeans and a white, V-neck T-shirt, his hair looking messier than normal. He shoots me a killer smile as his eyes find mine.

I'm a puddle of need and this man looks incredible.

He comes and sits on the bed next to me, lightly brushes my hair out of my face, and smiles. I'm sure it is a mess since I haven't done anything with it since I woke up. I swoon as he places a soft kiss on my forehead, and the last of my will power to take it slow disappears.

His eyes find mine and my lips find his. They are soft, but not demanding. He is gentle, working my mouth sweetly with his. I taste his coffee and worry about my breath since I didn't brush my teeth last night.

Liam shifts onto the bed with his back resting against the headboard as he pulls me astride him. I feel his desire through his jeans.

Am I ready for this? Why am I so hesitant?

I want him and he obviously wants me, but a nagging voice in the back of my head is telling me this isn't right. Not sure whether it is referring to the whole relationship or me sleeping with him.

I've been with him hundreds of times before, what would it hurt to take it to the next level now?

I make my decision and snake my hands under his shirt to pull it over his head. He looks at me and I nod. Next thing I know, he has the shirt I am wearing up and over my head. I am flipped around onto my back staring up at him. His blue eyes sparkle as they look down on me.

He lightly nibbles my ear and then starts trailing kisses down my neck, over my collar bone and gently begins pleasuring my breast with his mouth. His touches are sweet and light as he travels down further. Slipping off my underwear, he dives in.

With the help of his mouth, he brings me to the edge and over. I feel blissful and calm as he finishes undressing and sinks into me.

He moves slowly, kissing me as he takes his time enjoying every second. My mind jumps to the night I spent with Wren; the desire, the desperation, the fire. None of that is present, but it feels nice being with Liam.

Liam isn't fucking me like he had in the past; he is making love to me. The amount of passion I feel from him as he continues to move slowly starts to make me nervous. There are so many more feelings from him now than before. He releases my mouth, looking into my eyes. The words are there, but I will him not to say them. Not yet.

Deciding I need to take control before this leads somewhere I am not ready for, I roll us over so that he is below me and I begin to move, quicker.

His slow pace was holding me on the edge but not enough to tip either of us over. As I grind into him, I feel myself building quickly, bringing us both over the top quickly.

I fall back into the bed, breathing heavy. Liam knows what I did, and he looks over and smiles at me. "Soon, Jamie.

Very soon." He kisses me gently, then stands up and pulls his jeans back on but forgets about his shirt. With his tousled hair and bare chest, he looks delicious.

"I had them bring breakfast up. It may be cold now so we can either eat it or head down to eat in the dining room."

"I'm sure it's fine. Let me shower really quick and then I will be out."

I hop out of bed and scurry into the bathroom. Water turned up hot, I step into the shower and lean against the cold tiles. Why does everything have to be so complicated?

Just when I start to come around to the idea of being with Liam, he is ready to drop the big L word. Even though I thought I loved him before, I never told him, not wanting the pain of him not feeling it in return.

We aren't even in an official relationship yet! I haven't decided if I even want to be. Which is crazy because he is everything I've always wanted, but my brain keeps switching back to Wren.

Guilt settles into my stomach at the idea of what I just did and how I feel like I have cheated on Wren. If anything, it should feel the opposite. Whatever is between Wren and me is not a relationship.

Knowing I need to hurry up so Liam doesn't come looking for me, I use some of the hotel's soap to wash my hair.

Stepping out of the shower, I am determined to forget Wren and see where I stand with Liam. I think he could make me happy, and he really seems to care this time. We all make mistakes. I know I have made enough of them. I can forgive him for his. Everyone deserves a second chance, right?

After breakfast, Liam tells me to get dressed. He has something he wants to show me. As I am sitting in one of the hotel's robes, I realize that the only clothes I have is the nice dress I wore to dinner last night. I'm not sure what his plans are, but there are very few things that it would be appropriate for in this town.

As if reading my thoughts, he says, "You left a few things at my place, before. I brought them with me."

I send him a look. That's a pretty cocky thing to do when the last time I saw him I told him I wanted to take it slow.

He follows up quickly. "I was planning to return them to you. As much as I might have hoped you would stay the night, I didn't bring them assuming you would."

Still skeptical but glad I have something else to wear, I nod. He walks with me to the bedroom to grab the jeans and shirt and hands them to me. I turn my back and slip them on, wishing I had fresh underwear. I know for a fact that I had left at least one pair at his place in the past. What did he do with them?

Dressed in jeans and a flowy tank top, I turn to see Liam is the jeans and white shirt he had on earlier. I like the more relaxed look on him. I'm used to seeing him in suits and this makes him seem more like a real person.

He grabs his keys and we head to the door. I have asked a few times where we are going, but he says it's a surprise. We drive out of town, towards the road that leads to The Academy. Where is he taking me?

About halfway up the mountain where The Academy sits at the top, he flips on his blinker and turns down a road. Something about the road gives me déjà vu, but I don't ever remember being on it before.

Wren lives in the area just higher up the mountain, closer to The Academy.

Flipping the blinker again, he turns down a long, paved driveway. There must be a nice house at the end. The déjà vu grows and it all hits me when the house comes into view.

I know this house. I have been here once before—The Academy party that has haunted me since the night I attended it, along with Wren and our uncontrollable desire when we were in high school. That was the night I cheated on Mark. I'm not sure I will ever forgive myself.

My stomach becomes uneasy and breakfast threatens to come up. Why are we here? Why am I having such a bad reaction to a house?

Liam is smiling and I try to hide my discomfort because I can tell he is excited.

He gets out and then walks around to open my door. I get out and take his hand as he walks me toward the front door. I do my best to act natural, but this house brings back memories I would rather forget.

Liam opens the front door and walks in. It looks different than I remember. The whole interior has been redone and the furniture has changed. My discomfort fades since it's so different than it was before. I follow him into the living room.

He looks at me and asks, "What do you think?"

What do I think about what? It may be different, but my brain is still freaking out that this is *the* house that it hasn't fully grasped why we are here.

"About what?"

"The house. Do you like it?"

"It's a nice house." It is a nice house, but I would really like it if I didn't have the bad memories.

"I bought it."

My brain is still running in a million different directions and the words don't sink in.

"What?"

"I bought this house. I've fallen for this town and decided I want to move here. Obviously, I will have to travel and go down to the office occasionally, but you know I always did most of my work remotely."

Liam bought a house. In Accalia. Well, I guess it's past time we had the talk about where we stand.

Uncomfortable at being in this house again, Liam takes my silence the wrong way.

He grabs my hand. "Jamie, I know this is a lot and we will continue to take it slow, but I want to be with you. I'm tired of being a bachelor and I missed you every day when you were gone. I tried to forget you, I wanted to move on, but I couldn't.

"But that is not why I bought the house. During the time I have spent in Accalia, I I have found something I never thought I was looking for. Being so close to nature and seeing that view every day is everything I didn't realize I wanted."

I still haven't said anything, there are too many emotions going through my head, and I need a minute, or a year, to get them straight before I talk.

Liam holds my hand and leads me into the kitchen. "I had them stock the fridge so that we could have some food and wine here when I showed you."

He looks upset and I know it's because I haven't said anything yet. I need to say something.

Taking a deep breath, I give him a very generic overview of what happened. "I'm sorry. I'm happy for you, it's just that I've been in this house before and I don't have the fondest memories of the visit."

Liam looks concerned. "If you don't like it, I can sell it and buy another one. I want you to feel comfortable here."

"No, no, it's okay it's just a little bit of a shock. Give me a few minutes to adjust and I will be fine. I could use a glass of wine, though. We need to celebrate! You just bought a house!"

Feeling better already, Liam pours two glasses of wine and gets out a cheese platter. We take them out on the porch and enjoy the beautiful view.

Destiny

I can't help my thoughts drifting back to that night. The night that changed everything.

Chapter 25:

The longer I am in the house, the more I calm down. I've never had such a strong response to a place before. It was like my whole body had tensed up and it was hard to breathe. I have never had a panic attack before, but I imagine it would be like how I felt as the house came into view. The outside doesn't look like it has changed at all, but the interior has been completely redesigned.

The longer I sit here and the more wine I drink, the better I feel. Finally, I feel calm enough to acknowledge the other issue. Liam bought a house in the town I live in. Yes, it is a very nice town, but part of me doesn't believe him when he says the decision wasn't based on us.

As we have started to connect again, especially after this morning, I wonder how we could make this work. I'm back and I don't plan on leaving again. He is a CEO of a large company in the city and needs to travel for work. How would we possibly see each other?

He bought a fucking house.

We haven't even talked about if we are in a relationship. I'm just starting to warm up to the idea of us getting together, officially. What we had before was not a relationship. But since the day Liam showed up at the coffee shop, this has been everything I had hoped for and imagined when we were together before. Maybe the saying is true, absence makes the heart grow fonder. He never cared this much before, so why now?

Quite a few glasses of wine later, my filter has disappeared. "What are we?"

I catch him as he is putting a bite of cheese and cracker in his mouth. He chews thoughtfully chasing it with a sip of wine. "What do you want to be?"

Do I want to be his girlfriend? Titles always make everything complicated. But last time we left it very open-ended, and look how that ended up.

Feeling brave from the wine, I respond, "I feel like we deserve a proper chance. We both know what we had before was not a relationship."

He gives me a sideways look. "Jamie, did you just ask to be my girlfriend?"

"Who said I was asking?" I send him back a cocky smirk. God, alcohol can be great.

He chuckles and says, "All righty then, it's official, you're mine." He is everything I ever hoped for. Why am I not more excited by his words?

Maybe I need this to build my confidence after how we ended things. For better or worse, I am going to give it a try. Liam is a good guy; he will treat me right and support me. Or the new Liam will at least. Sometimes I forget they are the same person with how differently he acts. I wonder again what brought on this change.

I can worry later, now is the time to enjoy my new relationship. I crawl over to straddle Liam. "Why don't we make this official?" I run my fingers over the hard lines of his muscles under his shirt.

"You don't have to ask me twice."

His mouth finds mine. Most people don't get second chances, but I did, and I am going to make the best of it.

As I lay naked in bed next to Liam, I receive a text from Tollen asking what I am up to tonight. Not wanting to ignore my friend or Liam, I come up with a brilliant idea.

I want to show Tollen that I support her and Mark together, but I also don't want to be too obvious about it. The situation still has some strange feelings surrounding it, and while I think they would be happy together, they need to come to that conclusion on their own.

Liam is sitting at his computer, stark naked. I toss a pillow at him. "Are you okay if we do something with my friends tonight?"

He has been happier than ever since I agreed to be his

girlfriend. It makes me feel like we're doing the right thing, even if part of me is still pulling in another direction. Sometimes you just have to do what is best for you, not what you want most. Anything with Wren is just going to turn into a disaster, I just know it. Liam is stable, nice, and reliable.

"Of course, babe, whatever you want to do." Hearing him call me babe makes me smile. He never did that before.

As I turn back to my phone to text Tollen and Mark about meeting us in a few hours, I feel Liam shift on the bed. I feel his hand trail down my spine making me shiver. "How much time do we have before we meet up with them?"

"Long enough." I roll over and take his mouth with mine. It feels good to be with Liam, again. He knows what he is doing; he makes me feel cherished. There isn't the fiery desire I felt with Wren, but fire can be dangerous and is better left untouched.

Liam's hands explore my body as I feel the desire growing within me. He makes me happy.

I feel loved as he moves and slips into me. Every one of his actions is to make me feel loved as he devours my body. I know he can be rougher and more intense, but he doesn't seem to have any interest in coming together the way we used to.

Later in the day, we head into town to meet Mark and Tollen. I didn't tell either of them that the other was going to be there. Tollen told me she took Toby to her parents for the night, so they are kid-free and ready to have a good time.

Both of them want to meet Liam. I mentioned to Tollen that we were officially in a relationship, but I didn't tell her about him buying a house. It seems a little over the top and presumptive, but from when I worked for Liam, I have an idea of his finances and buying a house for him is like buying an expensive dress for me.

I told Liam to dress casually and he is in khaki shorts and a polo, about as casual as he gets. We pull up at the address I give him, and he looks at me with confusion. In front of us is a mini golf course, on the right is a huge rainbow slide, and on the left is a go-kart track. It is one of the two fun parks in town.

I give Liam a quick kiss on the mouth before I jump out of the car to join Tollen. "It will be fun!"

When I hug Tollen, she says, "I don't think I have come here since we were in high school." I know this is true for me. I wanted a fun environment for everyone to talk and hang out, and this came to mind. We will get food later, but there is only so much interacting to be had across a table in a restaurant.

Mark arrives last, eyes widening slightly when he sees Tollen, but hides any nervousness well. His smile is plastered on his face and he gives us both a hug. Tollen's is slightly more awkward. Mark shakes Liam's hand as I make introductions.

"I was thinking we could do a round of mini golf, followed by a few times down the slide, and maybe finish with the go-karts?" I tell them.

Everyone is shooting me skeptical looks, but they just nod.

I walk up to the counter and before I can move to pull out my wallet, Liam thrusts his credit card forward and pays for all of it. At least one thing never changes. He never used to let me pay for anything. I know I'm an independent woman and I should be fighting him for who's paying, but it's kind of nice to be taken care of.

Grabbing the golf clubs and balls, we head towards the green. This is going to be an interesting night.

―・―

Two hours later we are all laughing as Mark recollects the third round of go-karts we just finished. He won the first round and I the second; the third was to see who the overall champion would be. We were so busy trying to cut each other off that Tollen skirted around the edge and pulled ahead as the victor.

Liam seemed so out of his element when we started but is more relaxed now. I grab his hand and kiss his cheek. This is what I imagined when I thought about coming home, not the shitshow that everything has been up to this point.

Mark says to Liam, "Dude, you killed us at mini golf. Are you sure that is the first time you have played?"

He politely responds, "There wasn't a lot of time for 'fun'

growing up in my family. We had our sports, instruments, and languages to practice. My family wasn't very big on doing outings together." Just another reminder that Liam grew up in a very different world than us. I always thought that people with money had it all, but Liam seems to have missed out on so much.

Trying to pull the topic away from his family, which seems like a sore subject, I announce, "I think we need to make this a weekly thing, what do you guys think?"

Everyone nods in agreement and I mentally pat myself on the back for the idea.

Starving now, we all agree on Roy's, the local bar that also serves a mean burger. Mark offers to drive Tollen and a smile blooms across my face. They seem to be softening towards each other. I know the situation isn't ideal, but I really think they should give it a shot. As the afternoon progressed, they seemed to be less nervous about showing affection towards each other. Baby steps.

When we were golfing and I had Tollen alone for a moment, I told her about how Mark and I had dinner and that he told me about their relationship. I try to convince her I am okay with them being together, but she easily gathers some of my hesitation I can't seem to squash.

As I get into the front seat of Liam's black BMW, I look across the river that divides the parking lot from the park and see someone standing there. Looking at me.

It's Wren.

So, he's just going to follow me everywhere? What a creepy stalker.

I grab Liam's hand as he pulls away. I chose Liam so I need to forget about Wren.

As we drive towards the bar, though, I can't stop thinking about him. Everything is good, so why don't I feel happy? Will I ever be happy with what I have or will I always be wanting for something else?

Chapter 26:

A live band plays as I sit in the wood booth, drink in hand, leaning against Liam. Liam and Mark have really hit it off and are discussing something related to police forensics.

As the night has progressed, I've noticed Tollen moving closer and closer to Mark. He seems oblivious, but I can tell Tollen is trying to flirt with him.

A very upbeat song comes on. I finish the last little bit of my drink and grab Liam's hand. "Let's go dance." He looks uncertain but follows.

When we were together before, we always did what Liam wanted. Everything was structured and planned. Now, I have opened his eyes to a whole new list of activities today. He is doing better than I expected. I like how together he is, but sometimes you just need to let loose.

With his hand in mine, I get him to move to the music. He smiles and places a soft kiss on my lips. This is nice, there are so many things I missed about being home and now I have them, plus the guy.

I see Tollen has convinced Mark to get up and dance, too.

After a few fast songs, a slow one comes on and Liam pulls me into him. I am happy to see Mark and Tollen doing the same. Liam leans down and whispers, "This is really nice, Jamie. Thanks for giving me a second chance. I'm sorry for how I treated you before. It took you leaving for me to grow up and realize what I wanted."

I lean into his chest and hold him close. I'm glad I did, too.

Too soon, the night is over. We stayed on the dance floor for over an hour and only took a break to refresh our drinks. Mark, who stopped drinking over an hour ago, is driving Tollen home. They seemed to be getting closer over the night and I hope what is developing between them continues to grow. It would be perfect.

It's late and I expect Liam to take me back to his new house but am pleasantly surprised as we pull up in front of the hotel. It's just a house; I will get over it, but maybe not tonight. Whatever this is between Liam and me, I don't want something as silly as a house to cause a problem.

For tonight, I won't worry about it. Just enjoy the warmth I feel being with Liam. He has been so comforting and the perfect guy since he returned.

As we enter the hotel room, I push away everything else as I grab Liam's hand and lead him to the bedroom.

The next few days I am busy with work, but I continue to stay with Liam at the hotel. He can tell I am not ready to go back to the house yet and I appreciate him giving me the time I need. After stopping at my house for more clothes, I have been enjoying the luxuries of the hotel.

He says we wouldn't want to be at the house anyway since they have been moving in all of his stuff. I still can't believe he is moving here. I know he said it wasn't for me, but a small part of me likes the idea that it may have been.

I have texted Tollen a few times asking her about Mark, but she keeps dodging my questions. I know I am being pushy, but I want them to get together, officially.

The week has felt like a fairytale and I am sad that last night was our last night at the hotel. Liam has hinted that I should move in with him, but even with how well everything is going, I know it is too soon. Staying with him at the hotel felt so much less personal than at his house. I still want to take things slow and it's time I spent a few nights at my parents' house. Eventually I need to investigate getting my own place, but I will need to get a full-time job to be able to afford it. I love working with Roberta, but I am not making enough to pay rent on my own place.

I know Liam wants me to work with him again, but I think that will only end in disaster. What we have is working. I don't want to add working together into the mix. He makes me happy and I know it's soon, but I could see myself being with him. He is what you would call perfect husband material: stable, hardworking, and he adores me. But something is still nagging me that I shouldn't be with him.

Then there is Wren. I keep seeing him around, but he never tries to talk to me. It's like he is just watching me. I feel like he is protecting me, but I don't know what from. My dream from the night I got lost in the forest comes back to me and I remember the wolf howl that made my blood run cold. But if I was in danger, wouldn't he tell me?

The forests have slowly started to reopen even though they can't seem to track down what attacked the family. I keep having flashbacks to the night I found them. I'm not sure you are ever prepared to see a dead body, let alone one mauled by an animal.

The attack has been chalked up to a freak accident, but I know the park rangers are worried. My dad says that they have had no new signs of anything in that area and are just asking people to keep an eye out, stay aware. I hope this is the end of it, but I have a feeling that it's just the beginning.

Everyone seems to be moving past all these attacks quickly. Maybe I'm just hung up on them because of my brother. An unsettled feeling sits heavy in my gut.

I've stayed out of the forests, but I am beginning to miss them. I want to recommend Liam and I invite Mark and Tollen for a hike. If there are more of us, one with a gun, then we should be fine, right?

What if there are more attacks? How can people just move on when something is out there killing people?

Chapter 27:

I walk out of the coffee shop and take a deep breath as the summer sun hits my face. I've tried to stop thinking about Wren, I really have, but when I see him lurking and watching me it sets me on edge. Doesn't he have a job? How does he have time for it anyway?

A few days ago, I broke down and texted him, but I got no response. Yesterday I called, same. He is such a mystery.

I told Liam I needed to run an errand after I got off work today before I was going to meet him at his house, so I can track Wren down. Liam moved into his house a week ago. Once I am in the house it's fine, but I still feel panicked every time I drive up.

Wren can't keep ignoring me. I'm going to his house. I left work a few hours early since he seems to know my schedule. I asked my dad if he was working today and he isn't, so I figured I have a good chance of catching him. Also, the part I don't want to acknowledge is I miss him. We were becoming friends and then radio silence. Guys always complain that girls are moody, but I've never met anyone worse than Wren.

I pull out of the lot from the coffee shop and head towards his house. During the drive I try to think about what I want to say. What was the last thing we talked about? Why am I so nervous?

Before I know it, I am pulling into his driveway.

As I approach the house, I see his car and see it as a good sign that he is home. I put my car in park and take a deep breath. I want to pull down the mirror to check my makeup and hair. I resist. There is no reason for me to try to impress Wren, I'm with Liam.

Stepping out of the car, I head toward the front door. As I am about to knock, a branch cracks in the forest behind me. I spin around and investigate the trees but see nothing. Now hyper aware and on edge, I knock on the door, hard. I wait ten seconds, but it feels like an eternity. All the hairs on the back of my neck are standing up and everything is telling me I am in immediate danger. It reminds me of how I felt when I heard that wolf howl in my dream ... or was that a memory?

I test the handle and find it unlocked. I push it open, stepping in and slamming the door behind me. I'm breathing heavy and sweat starts to bead on my neck. What the hell?

Before I can fully catch my breath, I hear footsteps and Wren appears. His hair is wet and all he is wearing is a black towel tied around his waist. My calming heart rate speeds up again and I feel longing fill me that goes so deep I can't seem to stop it.

As if he feels the same, we rush towards each other, as if our bodies are being pulled together. Every cell in my body wants him. My breathing picks up again. I feel flushed and hot.

We end up face to face, only a few inches separating us. Since he is much taller than me, I am looking up at him. My body wants him so bad. Like two magnets being pulled together, neither of us seems to be able to resist. The vein twitches in Wren's neck as he holds himself back.

Liam.

His face flashes in my mind and I know I must resist. What we have is working and nice. I chose him and I need to stay committed. I put my hand on Wren's chest and immediately regret it as sparks shot through my body as if I am shocked by electricity. But instead of it hurting, it just increases the fire ready to explode inside of me.

I straighten my arm quickly, creating more room between us and then drop it quickly.

I clear my throat and look at him, "We need to talk. Go put clothes on."

The look I get in return tells me that putting on more clothes is the last thing he has on his mind. Whatever this attraction is between us is, it is not one-sided.

Without a word, he turns and heads in the direction of his room. I'm going to take that as a yes.

Remembering the layout of the house from the last time I

was here, I walk toward the living room. As I spot the couch, the memories come flooding back about the night we were together. It may not have ended well, but it was magical until then.

Squashing that idea, I head to the kitchen, hoping to find a cold drink to cool me down. There is a bottle of soda water in the fridge and I down half of it in one gulp. I tell myself it helps, but I still feel the desire burning inside of me.

I debate stepping outside to get some air but decide against it. I know something was watching me and I was in danger before I came into Wren's house.

That leaves the kitchen. I find a chair and sit down to wait for Wren.

I stare out the window and feel myself getting more nervous for Wren's arrival. The whole reason I have stayed away is because of this uncontrollable attraction, but I need answers. Now that I am prepared, it will hopefully be better.

After fifteen minutes, I pull out my phone and start scrolling through social media.

What is taking him so long? I know he was in the middle of a shower when I arrived, but it has been almost an hour with no sign of him.

Part of my brain keeps telling me he wants me to go find him. Maybe his restraint at the front door was just a pretense to make me feel comfortable, get me to let me guard down before he pounces.

I won't let him win.

I stay in the chair, about to text Liam that I am going to be later than I expected, when the front door opens. A few seconds later, Wren walks into the kitchen wearing his normal jeans, black shirt, and boots. Why was he outside?

He walks over to the fridge, grabs a soda water and downs the entire bottle. Then he finally turns to me and says, "Sorry, I needed to take care of something really quick." His hair is now dry and windblown, making me wonder what he was doing.

Not wanting him to realize how restless I've been while waiting for him, I try to act as nonchalant as possible. I take a sip of my now flat soda water and wait for him to talk first. He is keeping his distance, standing on the other side of the kitchen island. We both know we need to talk and that won't happen if we get too close.

Finally, he breaks the silence. "Hey."

"Hey."

"How are you?"

"Don't you already know since you have been keeping an eye on me?" The truth flashes in his eyes, he knows I have been spotting him.

"I wanted to make sure you were safe." Safe from what? My mind jumps to the bad feeling I had before I walking into Wren's house. Is there something out there that wants to hurt me that I don't know about?

"Safe from what?" Unable to stop myself, I ask more of the questions I have. "Why would I need to be watched when

I am in town and with other people? Is it related to the family that got attacked? What about the girl? What happened to her?"

Before I can ask more, Wren comes around the island, caging me between his arms using the counter to put his hands on. He isn't touching me, but I still feel the heat radiating off his body.

"You won't believe me if I told you. There are things out there, Jamie, that aren't good. I have been trying to figure out how to tell you, but you just keep running away from me."

"Well, I am here now. I came for answers and I am not leaving without them."

The heat between us is growing and I feel my will power cracking at his proximity. Just when I feel myself breaking, he pushes away and starts pacing.

"Jamie, I want to start by saying I am sorry. I really am sorry. Typically I am a very in-control person but something about you just riles me up, and not just on an attraction level. I guess that's a good place to start. I know the pull and need hasn't gone unnoticed between us. I feel it just as strongly, if not more than you do, but I have the benefit of understanding why. Do you want something else to drink? This may take a while."

I nod, not daring to say a word. He pulls out a bottle of wine and two glasses, pouring us each a large glass and staying with the island dividing us, again.

"All right, I'll start at the beginning. In 1887, there was a war going on between two villages. One was said to be the settlement that now makes up Accalia and the other was twenty miles south, near Periculum. Between the two was a place called Peaceful Valley, it is still called this today. This was a migration route for elk. Each settlement thought it was their land and fought endlessly over who got to hunt there.

"The settlement that sits where Periculum is now had heard of a lady with magical abilities, who lived in the mountains to the west, The Lady in the Woods. They were desperate and needed more meat to get through the winter ahead. The Lady in the Woods offered them a spell that would turn their warriors into wolves so they would have an advantage over the other settlement. She warned there would be consequences, but they agreed.

"The plan worked great, but then the other settlement struggled through the next winter, since they were unable to hunt the land with the elk without being killed. When spring came, they were desperate, so they made the trek to The Lady in the Woods. They asked for help so that they could be a fair match to their enemies.

"Shortly after, the leader of the Accalia settlement got sick and passed away. Some said it was the payment requirement for the magic. Everyone was scared and nobody wanted to lead, for fear that they would meet the same fate. The leader's daughter stepped up since nobody else would. Having a female leader at the time was unheard of, but she cared about the people and she could tell things were already starting to get disorderly without a leader.

"As winter approached, the war was heating up between the Acclia and Periculum, and both sides had lost many men. She took a chance and traveled to the valley with a group of Wolf Warriors to request a meeting with the leader of the other settlement. She had an offer to make that would hopefully bring peace to the two settlements.

"Two weeks later, they met to discuss a treaty. She stated that there was plenty of elk for both and fighting wasn't helping either of them. They would make an agreement for how many elk each side could hunt, leaving enough for both settlements to survive winter. She also inquired about the consequences they faced after the spell turned their warriors into wolves. He replied that nothing had happened. She was concerned by this, but let it go.

"The leader of the Periculum tribe said he had three sons and if she were to marry one of them, it would be her choice which son, then he would agree to the treaty. Seeing no other way, she agreed. One week from that day, he would travel with his three sons to the Accalia settlement.

"Upon their arrival, there was a celebration. Everyone wanted peace and it was finally going to happen. The Accalia leader's daughter was still uncertain, but decided that the choice was hers. All three of the boys had been given the ability to change into a wolf by The Lady in the Woods.

"The eldest son was very handsome, and everyone thought she would choose him. He was tall with blond hair and blue eyes. He was always set to lead his settlement when his dad passed away, but that could take a long time, so he was eager to oversee his own settlement.

"The middle son was burly and gruff. Having more muscle than brains. He was a good warrior, but not a good leader. His brown hair was messy, and he was not very intriguing to talk to.

"The youngest son was quieter but always had a look in his eye as if he was taking in everyone's conversation and making plans in his head. He was known more for sitting around reading or writing in journals than going out to fight. He was handsome, but in a more rugged way than his older brothers, with dark brown hair and light brown, almost yellow eyes. She was intrigued by him and found herself enjoying their conversation.

"At the end of the three-day celebration, she was to choose and be wed to the brother of her choice. Everyone expected her to choose the eldest brother, but she shocked everyone by choosing the youngest. She seemed happy and her mother could tell that she was falling in love with the boy. Although concerned by the arrangement, she was excited to see her daughter happy.

"The eldest was furious at her choice and chose to leave instantly to return home. The treaty was complete, and everyone was happy, except the eldest son. Each village had enough food for the winter and the settlements flourished.

"Ten years after the treaty was signed, strange disappearances and attacks started occurring in the Accalia settlement. Young women and men would go missing never to be seen again.

"Since there hadn't been any danger, and many of the warriors perished in the war between settlements, there were only a few people remaining in town with the gift to change into wolves. It was decided that they would run patrols at night to try and stop whatever was causing the disappearances and attacks. After a few weeks, the youngest brother joined the patrol. In the middle of the night, he came face to face with his older brother, whom he hadn't seen since the wedding.

"He was confused by his appearance until he saw the young girl on the ground bleeding. His brother was the cause of the recent disappearances and attacks. He had only a single question for his brother—why?

"His brother explained that a few years after they had last seen each other, he started to feel the wolf inside him clawing to get let out. Every week he would transform and hunt. One day, he traveled far and came across a group of travelers in the woods. After he had slaughtered them, he felt a calm like he had never felt before. The burning need to run and kill was absent for the first time in as long as he could remember. And he liked it. He liked the power killing another human gave him. Over the last few years, he had killed all the other Wolf Warriors in his town, including their other brother, because he felt they were a threat to his power. But he needed new people to hunt. Still mad at his brother for being chosen instead of him, he wanted payback.

"The youngest brother couldn't believe what his brother was telling him. In all these years, he had never felt this way, nor had any of the warriors left in his village.

"The youngest brother was torn; this was his brother, but he had evil in his eyes. He couldn't kill him, but he needed to get him away from both his people and those of the Periculum settlement. He banished his brother, sending word to his father, who was still alive and leading the other settlement, informing him of what had occurred.

"As the younger brother and his men banished his older brother, the elder brother turned around and said, 'You will regret this little brother.'

"Concerned for himself and his people, he traveled back to The Lady in the Woods. He was astounded that she hadn't seemed to age since the last time he journeyed to see her with his brothers. She explained that the Accalia settlement had paid their debt when the leader sacrificed himself. When asked, the leader of Accalia had accepted his death in payment for the Wolf Warriors, unlike the leader of the Periculum settlement. The wolf needed blood and since it wasn't given when asked, it took for itself.

"She also informed him that his children would be passed the gift of being a Wolf Warrior and the children of the other warriors. All would be men and they would carry the gene through their families. Females were not able to carry the warrior spirit, so it wouldn't be transferred to them.

"She warned that a bite or a scratch while in wolf form would lead to transferring the spell to those affected. Most would not survive; she gave great caution to not infect others. He thanked her for her help and headed toward the door. Before he reached it, it slammed shut.

"Surprised, he turned around. He saw the lady was now standing, but she looked different. Her hair was wild, and her eyes were rolled back into her head. She started speaking, but her voice was different than before.

"The evil will return, and he will have gained power and a following. The blood of the innocent keeps him young, but his rage never dies. A white wolf will be born out of wedlock and destined to be with your descendant. Their infernal connection will save the fall.

"After her premonition, she collapsed. Not knowing what to do, he brought her back to the Accalia settlement to nurse her back to health. After a week she awoke, grateful for his kindness. He insisted she stay a little longer to make sure she was all right. After another week, she had fallen in love with the town and decided to stay. She married one of the people in the settlement and she used her skills to help the youngest brother manage the young men that would transition into warriors when they hit puberty.

"They decided to start a school to help the boys adjust to this new side of themselves. They called it The Academy. Over the years, as technology began to increase, people stopped believing in magic and legends as freely, so they decided to keep the Wolf Warriors a secret.

"The Academy was and still is a sanctuary. Over the years, the word got out, and the youngest brothers' children learned that there were others like them out there and opened their doors to them as well. There was a similar academy on the east coast, but that was still a very fair journey at that day and age.

"Most Wolf Warriors were born, but there were some that had survived from scratches and bites. The Academy was a safe place for them to learn to control the warrior inside and teach them how to use it for good.

"The Eldest Brother was still alive but he kept his distance and he didn't bother The Academy, and kept moving so that they could never find him. He enjoyed killing and did it often. It was said that he located another witch who helped him extend his life, but the cost was taking the life of an innocent every month."

Pausing for the first time, he moves around the table, looking into my shocked eyes. He brushes my hair out of my eyes then says, "Jamie, you are the white wolf and I'm the descendant of the youngest brother. I know it sounds crazy, but we have been destined to be together since long before either of us were born.

"Both of the attacks that have occurred this summer, along with the one on your brother and his friends, are thought to be by the Eldest Brother. That is why I have been keeping an eye on you. He has returned. He is here for you, Jamie; he wants you."

Holy shit. I wanted answers and I got them. Everything he just told me is crazy, but a part of me tells me his words are true.

Chapter 28:

Two things keep circling in my head.

Wren said that I am a wolf. A wolf that was created out of wedlock.

Part of me has always known that there was something different about me. I'd always chalked it up to the typical doubt every teen and young adult holds.

I'm questioning everything I have ever felt. My pull to the mountains and Wren makes more sense.

I should be freaking out, but I feel calmer than I have in a while. I still need some time to think.

I stand up to leave. Turning to Wren, I say, "I need to go home and think this over."

Wren stands with me, looking worried. We have been sitting here in silence for a while and this is the first thing I have said.

Just to settle him, I add, "I believe you. It's crazy. *I'm* probably crazy, but it makes a weird amount of sense. I need a little while to wrap my head around it."

I move to grab my purse from where I set it when I walked into the kitchen. My body feels like it is floating above reality, not really sure where to land. I'm a wolf, or a wolf warrior, as Wren called it. What does this mean?

Wren follows me as I walk towards the door, careful to keep some distance between us, but close enough that I know he is there.

As I reach the door, I turn around and lean my back against it. Wren stops a foot away, staring into my eyes. I focus on his yellow-brown eyes for a moment and it hits me.

The black wolf. It's Wren.

He sees the realization form in my eyes and nods as if confirming my thought.

So many questions have been answered, yet I'm more confused than ever. He said that the prophecy stated we were destined for each other, but what if I just want a normal life? Is a normal life possible for me?

My thoughts drift to Liam and his normalcy. If everything Wren told me is true, if I really am a wolf, could I be with him without putting him in danger?

My eyes are still on Wren as I say, "I should leave."

"Are you sure that's what you really want to do?"

My body is telling me to stay, but my brain screams at me to run away as fast as I can. I never did like being told what to do, even if it is destiny speaking.

I reply with a curt, "Yes."

I open the door. As soon as I'm outside, the earlier feeling of being watched returns. I scan the area and find no one, but I can't seem to brush it off.

Wren approaches, obviously sensing my unease from the way he's looking around. *Of course,* he's the wolf. I don't know how I didn't notice it before. Everything about him is primal, wild, right down to the way he scans his surroundings like a predator stalking his prey. "I thought I scared him off, but he must have returned. I'm not leaving you alone. We can either stay here or I will come with you to your parents' house. Your choice?"

Why is he always telling me what to do?

I ignore him and head to my car. He follows without saying anything and gets into the passenger seat.

My phone dings and I look down to find a text from Liam. *Hey Babe, what time should I expect you so I can plan dinner?*

Shit. Liam. I completely forgot.

I send him a quick text that something has come up and I will need to go to my parents for the night. I can't face him right now.

I pull out of Wren's driveway, my brain swirling with what he's told me. I'm shaking as we wind down the road.

Suddenly, something jumps out in front of the car. Wren shouts something as I slam on the brakes. The car fishtails one way then rights itself before coming to rest inches from a guardrail.

Gripping the steering wheel tight, I strain to see into the dark forest. My heart is beating like crazy.

It was a wolf. I know it. And I have a feeling it didn't jump out in front of my car by accident.

For the first time, I'm scared. Something or someone out there wants to cause me harm and I have no way to protect myself.

Wren puts a comforting hand on my arm. "Let me drive."

I nod without argument and we switch sides.

After adjusting the seat, he continues down the road. I stare out the window, not sure what to think or how to feel.

We pass Liam's driveway, and I peer up at the dark house on the hill and sigh. The last few weeks with him have been amazing and so normal, but I have a feeling that things will never be normal again.

The night is a blur. I ate dinner with my parents and Wren but stayed silent and didn't follow what they were talking about. I'm in shock and mad at them for not telling me. They must have known. Wouldn't they?

I caught my mom and Wren having a hushed conversation earlier, but they stopped as soon as I walked into the room. I need to take tonight for me and then I will confront them tomorrow.

Wren is a wolf. I am a wolf. We are destined for each other.

My brain keeps circling through everything I've learned. There is still a part that doesn't believe what he's told me. No one would blame me for saying he is crazy and never talk to him again. I almost wish I could. Forget everything I just learned and spend my life with Liam. A normal life.

As I lie in bed, I can't seem to slow my brain down. To add to everything, Wren is sleeping in the room next to mine. How am I supposed to sleep knowing he is so close?

After what feels like hours of staring at the ceiling, Moon barks outside. She doesn't do it often, so it instantly makes me concerned. I get up quickly and follow the sound of her bark.

She is standing by the back door pawing hard at it. She's really upset and obviously wants to be let outside.

As I debate what to do, I feel someone approach. Wren is standing there in just his tight black boxers. I quickly find his eyes, so I don't look at his naked chest.

He walks up to the window and looks out. The way he scans the forest makes me think that he can see much better than me, since all I see is darkness.

"Stay here, Jamie."

Before I realize what is happening, he opens the door and runs out.

It happens so quickly, I barely catch the transformation, as he changes into a wolf and bounds across the lawn—the black wolf I saw in the forest, the one I felt a connection to but didn't understand why.

He is both beautiful and terrifying as he disappears into

the trees that line my backyard.

Without thinking, my feet begin to move, and I chase after him. It feels natural, instinctual. Only wearing a t-shirt and boxer shorts, I dodge into the dark forest.

Moon barks again and I follow the sound. She sounds upset and I'm worried something has happened to her.

As I follow her barks, I leave the trees and enter a clearing. Moon is standing in the middle of it, barking at a wolf. It is huge. Light brown, almost blond fur, and when he looks up at me, his blue eyes shine in the dark night.

With one quick swipe of his paw, he knocks Moon out of the way and hurtles toward me.

Why did I run out here with nothing to protect myself? I look around but there is nothing, not even a stick or rock within reach for me to fight back.

I know I won't be able to outrun him, so I stand there, helpless, as he covers the distance between us much too quickly. I feel a tingling in my extremities like something is trying to claw its way out of my skin.

He stops a few feet away and just stares at me. Where Wren's eyes are soft, this wolf has hard, savage eyes. They drill into me as he takes me in slowly, scanning me from head to toe.

Every hair on my body stands on end. I've never been more terrified in my life. As I prepare to be attacked, another howl comes from my right. The wolf with the blue eyes swipes at me, throwing me backwards just as there is a rush of air.

Before he can advance, Wren flies into his side and knocks him away.

On the cold, hard ground, I watch the two wolves tumble together as they fight. They growl and throw themselves at each other, their teeth bared.

I want to get up, to help, but I'm immobile. A stinging sensation courses through my forearm. Moon comes limping over to me and lays her head in my lap. My body feels hot, as if something is burning inside of me.

Moon licks my arm. I look down and see a small scratch.

The last thing I think before I pass out is, *I am going to die. Just like that little girl.*

Chapter 29:

Pain. Burning. Heaviness crushing me.

I'm in hell and I can't get out. Drowning in a pit of fire as I am crushed by an invisible weight.

My blood burns through my body. I'm dying. I don't want to die.

I fight. I push against the feeling, clawing my way to the edge. Freedom. I need to get away from here.

I don't know where out is, but I fight with everything I can to get to it.

Jamie. Jamie. Jamie.

My name echoes off the black walls surrounding me. I focus on it and push towards it.

A gasp leaves my mouth as I shoot up to sit. Immediately, I regret moving. Everything hurts. What happened? Where am I?

The bed or cot I am laying on is hard, a metal pole digging into my butt. I look around at the concrete walls, and the bars that line one side. Where am I, in a cage?

The heat is gone, and I immediately feel cold as my sweat-soaked body adjusts to the cool air. I begin to shake, feeling tears prick in the corner of my eyes. I'm scared.

A small voice comes from the bars. "Are you cold, miss? I have a blanket and water if you would like them."

I look over to see a boy. He can't be older than ten, with a mop of blond hair and blue eyes. He sits with his feet propped on a container as he reads what looks to be a comic book. I'm not sure what is going on, but I am freezing and thirsty, so I take his offerings. Wrapping the blanket tightly around myself, I open the bottle and down it in one swig. "Where am I?"

The boy is about to answer when a door slams open and footsteps pound toward me. My heartbeat again spikes through the roof. I look around, but my cell has nowhere to hide, so I pull the blanket in tighter and hide my face in my knees, sure I'm about to die.

Someone calls my name as the metal bars clink. Before I can look up, I'm pulled into a tight embrace. Wren. I know him without seeing him. The warmth from his body sinks in immediately. All the tension I have been holding fades as the tears begin to fall. In his arms, everything feels right.

After a few minutes, I look up into those light brown eyes I love. Wren is here, everything will be okay.

He pulls back slightly to look in my eyes. There is so much concern on his face I almost start crying again, but I struggle to hold myself together. If I keep crying, he won't be able to explain what is going on.

Keeping one hand securely around me, he uses the other to swipe the sweat-drenched hair out of my eyes. As he begins to talk, I feel his chest rumble. "Jamie, god Jamie, I thought I had lost you."

What happened?"

He pulls me in tightly and just rocks me softly, further calming me. This feels so right. Being here in his arms, in this moment.

The silence is broken when the boy mutters, "Are you guys going to start making out or something? I'm not supposed to leave, but I really don't want to watch that. Gross." I had completely forgotten he was here.

Wren chuckles. "Hey Andre, why don't you tell everyone she is awake? I will help her get cleaned up and then bring her down to the dining room."

Andre grabs his comic and responds as he begins to run up the stairs. "Sounds good, bro. Glad your girl didn't die."

His girl?

He shifts and scoops me up. I want to argue, but I feel so weak I don't know if I can walk upstairs right now.

I'm still wrapped up in the blanket as he carries me out of the cell and up a dark, stone, spiral staircase. It's as if we are in a real-life dungeon.

Shifting me to one arm, he opens the door and enters a large hallway. Light streams in from a large bay window that frames the mountain. I lean my cheek against Wren's chest. As I look down the hall, I think I see a mop of red hair move around the corner.

A flash of recognition hits me, but I shake my head. It can't be. I'm so exhausted, I'm making things up in my head.

It hits me as he moves me through the building, the old arched stone doorways, the stately, dark-wood paneled columns, and the tapestry-covered walls, that we are in The Academy, but Wren hasn't said a word since we left the basement.

He stops at a door. "Can you stand?"

I nod, hoping I'm not overestimating myself. I already feel like a damsel in distress, and the last thing I need is to collapse in front of Wren.

On shaky legs, I stand with one of Wren's arms still supporting me as he fishes a key from his pocket and turns it in the lock. Then he helps me into the room.

I look around and notice the much more modern touches than the rest of the building. Wren leads me to the huge bathroom.

Wren sits me down on a chair. "Bath or shower?"

There is a beautiful standing shower lined in white tiles, but it's the bathtub calling me. "Bath." I say, not wanting to admit that I don't think I can stand long enough to take a shower.

After Wren turns on the water and pours something in that fills the bathroom with the smell of lemongrass, he squats down in front of me, just looking at me.

He takes a deep breath. "I bet you have a few questions. I'll answer them all. I'm just so happy that you are alive, I'm still in shock. A female has never survived the transformation. I had hope since your dad has the wolf spirit, and according to the legend, you are the white wolf. But, after five days, I started to lose hope when you didn't wake up. There is something very special about you, Jamie Carter."

I clear my throat because it still feels like sandpaper. "I was out for five days?"

Wren fills a glass with water and brings it to me. "Jamie, it's been two weeks since the night in the forest." He must see the shock on my face, but he continues before I can say anything else. "Let's get you into the tub and then I will explain the rest."

Wren stands up and starts by helping me grab the blanket I still have tucked around me. As I look down, I realize I'm still wearing the boxers and t-shirt I had on when I ran out into the forest after Wren. That is the last thing I remember, other than the feeling of burning.

As Wren reaches to help me with my shirt, I hesitate for a second. After this, I feel so connected to him, but I am still with Liam.

He sees me hesitate and says, "Nothing will happen, Jamie, I promise, but you need my help. Let me help."

I see how much he needs this, and I don't feel strong enough to do it on my own, so I let him. As he is helping me,

I notice a bandage on his arm. What happened to the other wolf? Was it the Eldest Brother? Why does he want me?

After Wren helps me out of my clothes, he supports me as I make my way over to the bathtub. The little energy I had seems to have disappeared and I feel exhausted. As I try to climb into the tub, I struggle and slip. Wren catches me, holding me up.

"Dammit Jamie, be careful." He sets me so I am sitting next to the bathtub and quickly begins to undress.

I am too tired to argue, let alone get in the bathtub. As he peels his shirt over his head, I see a large, raw scratch down his chest.

I reach out without thinking and run my fingers along it. Wren flinches with my touch and I worry I've hurt him.

He finishes pulling off his pants and gets into the bathtub with me. "I was able to hold him off until others came. What were you thinking, running out there after me? When I entered the clearing and saw you there, my heart shattered. I thought I had lost you. I can't lose you."

"Who was the wolf with the icy eyes?" I ask. As Wren gently helps me wash the sweat and grime that is coated to my skin, he fills me in.

He tells me the wolf that attacked me was the Eldest Brother, but doesn't give me any more details. After back-up came, they chased him for hours but were never able to catch up to him. He was fast. Since I had been scratched, they brought me back to The Academy. Nobody knew what would happen. Traditionally females don't survive twenty-four hours after they've been infected. It isn't that females are weaker; it is because the spirit originated from a male, or so the folklore says. For a female to survive, she must fight twice as hard as any male.

After I survived the first day, there was hope. I had been placed in the cell in case I transformed. Typically within 48-72 hours after being infected, you either die or transform. I did neither. According to Wren, I was in a fevered haze for the remainder of the two weeks. They tried to give me an IV, but I was writhing so much, I wouldn't let them. Wren stayed by my side most of the time.

My parents and Liam have no idea where I am. At some point, I am going to have to tell them. How do I explain what happened? What can I explain?

I'm awake and alive. Nobody thought I would make it this far, so there is no plan moving forward.

After I am clean and dressed, Wren offers to go down to get me food from the cafeteria. I want to see more of The Academy and learn more about what I am, but I'm too tired to focus.

I fall asleep almost instantly when Wren leaves.

The sound of the door reopening stirs me from my dream. Shortly after, I feel a warm hand rubbing my arms trying to rouse me.

"Hey Jamie, I need you to eat a little. Then you can go back to sleep."

Slowly, I open my eyes. It has gotten dark outside. Wren sets a large tray filled with more food than I could ever eat on the table.

He sits next to me and says, "I didn't know what you would want so I grabbed a little bit of everything. Sorry it took so long, everyone wanted to talk about you."

"Everyone … who?"

"You'll see. If you are up to it in the morning, you can come down to breakfast. But I told them it might take a few days."

I nod and look over the food Wren brought. I grab a bowl of chicken noodle soup with a slice of bread. My stomach is uncertain for the first few bites, but then I become ravenous. I devour the soup and move to a bowl of pasta. Finally, I finish with a bowl of fruit and sit back, stuffed.

Wren is smiling at me, silent. I give him the, *what's up?* look.

"It's good to see you eat. I know I have already said it a hundred times, but I was so worried the last two weeks. It has been torture. All I could do is watch you suffer as you tossed and turned." He pauses for a moment, looking like he wants to add more then he shrugs, stands up, and offers me a hand. "Why don't we get you to bed?"

My eyelids are already dropping as he leans down to pick me up. I feel safe against his warm chest and never want him to let me go.

As my head hits the pillow, I enter the oblivion of sleep. I don't know what my life will be like tomorrow, but for the moment, I am safe and content.

Chapter 30:

The morning sun streams through the window and hits my face. My eyes flicker open, and I lie there, stretching. I have more energy. My muscles are weak and my skin raw as if it has been burned from the inside out, but I'm not the zombie I was yesterday.

I'm alive and I'm a wolf, or at least I think I am. I don't fully understand everything that is going on. Supposedly, I was born a wolf, yet I have never transformed and now I have been scratched, but didn't change. I didn't physically transform, but I feel as if I was reborn. All my senses are heightened and the world looks different. I'm different. Now that I am aware of it, I feel the wolf inside me. It was always that inner voice that I kept hearing, but she is louder now. The side pushing me to return to the mountains. She is trapped and I don't know how to let her out.

As I become more conscious, I'm slowly made aware of the warm, hard chest my head is laying on. I run my hands over the contours of muscles and hear a purr come from Wren. I look up and find his eyes.

He looks tired. The last two weeks have taken a toll on him as well. What is worse? Living the hell or watching someone you care about go through it?

He runs his hand up and down my arm. "How did you sleep last night?"

"Good. My body still feels beat, but not as much as last night."

"Think you have enough energy to head down to breakfast? If we don't go down soon, everyone is going to break down our door."

His words ring in my head, *our door.* Are we an *our*?

The last two weeks have felt like a dream. The whole realization that I have blood running through my body that will help me turn into a wolf is still new and I need time to adjust. But I can't wait forever. "All right."

Wren leans in and kisses me on the forehead. Desire instantly floods me.

I push myself off Wren's chest and get out of bed, a task made difficult by my beat-up body.

Once showered and dressed, I almost feel normal. My hand moves to my necklace, the moonstone I bought right after returning to town, it feels warm against my neck. I feel comforted when I place my hand on it and wonder if I was drawn to it because of it being a moonstone. I definitely lost weight over the last two weeks. I catch a glimpse of Wren's scratch as he is pulling his shirt down. It looks better than it did last night.

Without thinking, I walk over and run my fingers over the outline of it through his shirt. "Does it hurt?"

He doesn't wince as I touch it, but I know he tries to be tough, so I don't know how he feels. "Not much anymore. The first few days it burned from the infection of the wolf claws but it's better now. Unfortunately, it will leave a scar. The Wolf Warriors heal faster than normal, but injuries that are sustained from other wolves don't completely disappear like others." He pauses and then asks, "You up to walking down to the cafeteria?"

"Yeah, sure."

The stairs take me longer than I would like, but I make it down. Now that I am more with it, I can take the time to really look at The Academy. I have always seen it from a distance, but I didn't realize how big it was. Large open hallways made of stone are lined with paintings. Most of which depict wolves in battle, wolves with humans, and all of them are set in the lush forests that surround this area.

I'm stopped when I see a small painting hanging by itself. I find myself staring when Wren comes up behind me. "That is a painting of the youngest son and his wife, the daughter of the leader to the Accalia settlement. This was said to have been painted right after they opened The Academy. It was much smaller back then but, over the years, it has been expanded to the size it is today. If needed, we could house one hundred people here. Mostly, The Academy is for boys that, by birth or by attack, find themselves with the wolf spirit running through their blood, but we take in anyone that needs a place. If the need exists, we also take in the siblings of the ones that are affected. Those are the females that attend The Academy."

I hear what he is saying, but my eyes have not left the painting. They are about ten years older than Wren and I are now, but the resemblance is uncanny. I am looking at an older version of Wren and myself.

I think back to the story Wren told me. He is a descendant of the brothers, but he said I was from another spirit line, born out of wedlock. It doesn't make sense. My parents were married when they had me, maybe the prophecy isn't totally accurate.

We are interrupted by a door opening down the hallway. A group of teenagers walk out, all but one of them boys. When I think back on it, I realize most of the people I saw from The Academy were boys.

When the group of teenagers sees us, they stop and stare.

Wren breaks the silence. "Jamie, I'd like you to meet some of the students that live here at The Academy. Jack, Matt, Brad, Chloe ... this is Jamie."

They keep staring. After a few awkward moments, the tall one in the back with dark hair says, "I'm glad you are finally here. Maybe Wren will be less cranky now that he's getting laid."

The kids laugh. Shocked, I don't know how to respond to him.

Wren jumps in. "Jack, don't you have some new agility moves to practice? Last I remember, you were getting destroyed by Matt."

The boy slumps slightly and murmurs something I can't hear. As they all shuffle past us, I notice the way Chloe stares at Wren. I feel my stomach roil with jealousy. *Back off bitch.* I stifle a growl from coming from my throat, but when she catches my eyes, she turns away instantly, redness creeping into her cheeks.

Wren grabs my hand and leads me to the double doors at the end of the hall. All the doors in this hallway are tall and wooden, extending up to the vaulted ceiling. I feel as if I am in a medieval castle.

As we open the door, conversation flows. We're in a large room with a massive stained-glass window of a group of wolves in the forest. They have to hide everywhere else; this is their sanctuary where they can be themselves.

As we enter, everyone stops talking. The room becomes eerily quiet. We just stand there as every set of eyes watches us. I feel like prey about to get pounced on.

A chair scrapes and an older gentleman walks toward me. A flash of familiarity hits me, but I can't place it. His hair is dark brown and peppered with grey. As he approaches, I get a better look. When I see his eyes, I know instantly who he is. I pause, frozen in time, not wanting it to be true, but I can't deny what is standing right in front of me.

As he reaches us, he holds out his hand. I reach out tentatively to take it. "Jamie, I am so glad that you've recovered. We were all so worried. This is new territory for all of us and we felt helpless, not knowing what to do. My name is Edward, and I would like to formally welcome you to The Academy. I am the headmaster here. Please, never hesitate to come to me with questions. If you choose, you will always have a home here. I know that all this may seem like a lot. If I had my way, we would have told you from the beginning, but your mom wanted you to have a traditional upbringing. I am here if you ever have any questions."

I know the answer, but I ask anyway, to get confirmation. "You're my father?"

My body has gone through so much shock lately that it struggles to handle this new piece of news. The floor threatens to fall out from underneath me. Wren's arm comes around me to steady me.

He nods, "Yes, Jamie, I am your father. My blood runs through your veins. I will never try to replace your dad, but I have watched you grow up and I am very proud of you."

He looks behind me, then nods and walks away. Trying to grasp the full impact of what I've just discovered, I focus on taking a few deep breaths to steady myself.

I look up to find my mom standing in the doorway looking around. Her eyes catch mine and she runs over.

After the ups and downs of the last few weeks, I find comfort in my mom's arms. She starts crying and telling me how happy she is that I am okay.

With my arms around her, I say only so she can hear, "You have a lot of explaining to do."

Chapter 31:

After breakfast, Wren takes my dad on a tour of The Academy while I go back upstairs with my mom. She is quiet as we make our way to the room I stayed in last night with Wren.

How do you start a conversation like this with your mom? With anyone, for that matter?

This doesn't change that my dad will forever be my dad. He has been there for me every day of my life and I feel bad for what my mom put him through. Does he know? With no better place to start I say, "Does dad know?"

She looks upset and embarrassed, as she should be. "Yes, honey, he does. I never stopped loving your dad. I just lost my way for a little while. It was a mistake, but it gave me you, so I will be forever grateful." She pauses, and I wonder if she had a similar pull to Edward that I feel with Wren.

Before I can ask, she continues, "After your father and I had your brother, we always wanted more kids, but sometimes wanting just isn't enough. We tried for years but never had success. When we went to the doctor, she said it was me. I wasn't producing enough progesterone, so the eggs weren't viable. I became depressed.

"Then I met Edward in town at the coffee shop. We started off as friends and became more. After a few months, I came to my senses and cut it off, spilling everything to your father. He had suspected, but never said anything. He is such a kind and understanding man, we were able to work through it, under the condition that it was over. We had Jacob, who was almost ten and this is when I decided to go back to work.

"We didn't realize I was pregnant until I was four months along. It was a miracle and we were grateful. We never did a paternity test, but when you came out with Edwards eyes, we both knew. Your dad never mentioned it and always treated you as his own.

"I hadn't had contact with Edward in months, but I felt he deserved to know. I showed up at The Academy and as I was pulling up, I watched one of the younger boys change into a wolf then run into the forest. I was so shocked, I just sat in my car until Edward came out. That was the day he explained everything to me, including the prophecy.

"All I wanted was for you to grow up and have a normal life. That was why, when you were interested in The Academy, we told you we couldn't afford it. I saw little things that happened, like your temper and attitude that hinted at the wolf inside you, but I kept hoping he was wrong. When you moved away, it was hard for us, but I hoped it would lead to you living a normal life."

She breaks down in tears and pulls me into her. "I thought I lost you, baby. I don't think I can survive losing another child."

She has known all along. She knew it wasn't some random animal that killed my brother. It was a wolf. Did he get attacked because of me?

"What happens if I can't transform into a wolf? Why haven't I transformed?"

I have always been aware of something trapped inside of me. I never knew what it was and assumed it was normal. I knew deep down there was always something different about me, but I never in a hundred years expected this.

My mom puts her hand on my arm. "Honey, nobody really knows. This is new territory for everyone, but we are all here to support you."

The door opens. Wren and my dad come in. I haven't gotten a chance to really talk to my dad, so I stand up, walk over, and he pulls me into a hug.

"Hey munchkin, how are you holding up? You gave us a mighty scare there. Your mom and I are getting older and our hearts can't handle the stress. Let's not have any more near-death experiences, okay?"

I love the feeling of being in my dad's arms. He has always been there to pick me up when I have fallen. "I love you, Dad. I will always love you." I don't have to say more, he understands.

My dad clears his throat and I can tell he is close to tearing up but holds it back. "I love you too, Jamie Bear. I think we have taken up enough of your time, but we just wanted to see with our own eyes that you were okay. Call me if you need anything."

With that, he grabs my mom's hand and they walk out of The Academy. I watch them from the window as they drive away. Edward is standing on the front stairs, watching, too. I wonder if he has never gotten over my mom.

What do I do now? My life has been flipped upside down and I don't know where I stand. I call Liam; he is extremely worried, but he can hear that I am okay. He wants to see me, but I tell him I need a few days to recover before I feel up to it. I hear the love in his voice, and it makes it hard to deny him.

I still care about him, but I don't know if, after everything, I can be with him. He doesn't deserve to be dragged into this crazy world. But I still want him. I still like the idea of having a normal life with him. Simple days filled with work, love, and eventually kids.

Part of me thinks this is possible. The wolf hasn't emerged in me and may never come out. Even if it did, from everything I have learned, it's voluntary when you transform. I could live a normal life with him.

Then there is Wren. He has been nothing but kind and

tender with me lately. Never pushing anything and just being there for me. But with Wren comes this lifestyle. I can tell, even during the few days I have been here, that he is an important member of The Academy and the wolf community. He is very respected by the students and the other teachers. I've learned a lot about him in the last few days. His job is to help the new students cope with their new reality. Some of the kids have known they're wolves since birth, but many of the kids who show up at The Academy are taken by surprise. They have either been born to unknowing parents or they were infected. Apparently, the wolf spirit chooses who it wants to stay with, as it has been known to skip generations.

Puberty is bad enough. Imagine finding out you're a wolf.

Wren tells me he came here when he was twelve years old. Other than the small amount of information he gave me when we first met, I know nothing about his past. He doesn't seem very open to sharing it either.

Tollen is super worried about me since I basically dropped off the face of the planet for two weeks, but I don't have any extra energy to deal with her questions. I ignore her calls and send short text replies. We were just starting to regain our friendship, I hope this doesn't ruin that.

I've been here a week and finally people have stopped staring at me. Everyone knows about the prophecy so there is a lot of talk about Wren and me. We are always together, but we haven't taken it past friends, and I am grateful he is giving me time to think.

It's been very calm, and it seems the wolf that is hunting me has disappeared for now. I'm not naive enough to believe he is gone, but there are forty-seven wolves total in The Academy and surrounding area. Returning is suicide.

Since the incident, the wolves have started patrolling the woods around the town. They knew he was a threat before, but didn't think he would be this bold. Something has changed recently, causing him to risk the return. I know it has something to do with me, but I feel like everyone is still holding back a part of the story I don't know.

That's a future problem. Today, I want to see Liam and see where we stand. He knows I have been at The Academy with Wren for the last three weeks. I need to explain we are just friends and hope he will listen.

Looking at the clock, I realize he will be here any minute to pick me up. I wanted my parents to bring my car here, but Wren didn't like the idea. He said I still need to rest, and wants to be able to decide when I can leave. Not sure what he thinks gives him permission to boss me around. He doesn't know Liam is coming and I am trying to keep it that way.

I head for the back door, hoping to slip down the backstairs to make a stealthy retreat. As I open it, I come face to face with Wren.

Tilting his head to the side slightly, he says, "You look really nice. What is the occasion?"

Before today, I hadn't bothered with my appearance. I basically died. I think that gives me the right to take the week off. But I am already on thin ice with Liam so I am hoping if I look cute, it will help my case.

Looking back at Wren, I realize I am not going to get out of here without an explanation, so I give one. "I'm going to town to get coffee with a friend." It's not a lie, it's just not the whole truth.

He looks concerned. "Are you sure you are up to that?"

Now more than ever, I want a ordinary life. I can't deny there is something between Wren and me, but there are two huge things working against anything happening between us. First, I would be following the prophecy or destiny or whatever, and I hate being told what to do. Secondly, if I am with Wren, I am going to be fully immersed in this world. I've only seen parts of it for a short time, and I can already tell it is a crazy one, full of twists and turns.

"Yes. I feel okay. I have been cooped up here all week; it would be nice to get out for a little while."

There is concern in his face, but he says, "Okay. Just take it easy and let me know if you want me to come and get you. Also, go to Roberta's coffee shop, she can keep an eye on you."

It suddenly hits me. "Roberta knows about the wolves, doesn't she?"

He nods but doesn't elaborate.

As I walk by Wren and head down the stairs, I think about how different Wren has been this past week. He has been nothing but caring and sweet, a drastic contrast to the moody and closed off man I had become accustomed to. The pull is still there, but the more time we spend together, it seems to lessen the intensity. I think how we have been sharing a bed every night and start to feel guilty. I don't want to lead Wren on, but I feel safe when I am closer to him.

Chapter 32:

Liam pulls up as I am exiting. His flashy, black BMW convertible still looks out of place among the mountains, but it fits him so well. He hops out of the car and pulls me in for a deep kiss. I stiffen, not because of the kiss, but because of where we are. This area is very open and we probably have multiple sets of eyes on us at the moment, including Wren's.

Feeling my hesitancy, he pulls back and looks at me with his icy blue eyes. "Is everything okay?"

I nod and respond, "Considering how shitty the last few weeks have been, yes, but this is just a really public area."

He seems to understand, and being the perfect gentleman, opens the passenger-side door for me.

When he gets in the car, he says, "I have been extremely worried about you. I know we just recently restarted our relationship, and I can't apologize enough for how I treated you before, but I like what we have. I love you, Jamie, and eventually I would like to marry you." My jaw drops.

He sees my shock, so he adds, "I don't expect you to say anything right now, I just needed to say it."

Being honest with him, I reply, "Liam, I care about you, too, and I want to make this work, but there are a few things I need to figure out with my life right now before I can head down the road to that type of commitment."

Liam smiles at my response. It wasn't a hell yeah, but it wasn't a no, either. "Jamie, I want to be with you. Whatever it is, we will figure it out."

With that, he pulls out of The Academy parking lot. I tell myself not to look back. There is no reason to look back, but as we approach the corner that will take the view of The Academy away, I peer over my shoulder to see Wren standing on the deck in the front of the building, watching me.

We are a few hundred feet away from him, but I can tell from his hunched stance that he isn't happy. It makes me second-guess the choice I made to return to Liam, I feel a new warning voice I never noticed before. Something is making me feel uneasy when I look at Liam's eyes. I'm determined to give it a chance,my heart is still telling me that the road with Wren will be bumpy and dark. I just want a normal life.

I turn around, trying to enjoy the warm summer day. Before we know it, the snow will return, and winter will be here. Don't get me wrong, I love the snow, but there is something about the warm sun on your face with the cool mountain breeze that just settles my soul.

I just need to take it one day at a time right now and not

worry about the future.

After about twenty minutes of Roberta gushing over me, Liam and I head out to my table on the porch, drinks in hand.

I don't know what Liam knows or where to start, so I awkwardly begin, "I know the last few weeks have been strange. Not only for you, but also for me. A lot of things have changed in my life recently and I am still trying to wade through it all. You have already been incredibly patient with me and I appreciate it, I really do, but just give me a little more time."

Liam nods. "Are we still together?"

With these words, I know I have an out. This would be the perfect time to tell Liam it just isn't working right now. I should do it for Liam. Free him of me and my crazy life. But I can't do it. I don't know how we will make it work, but I want to try.

I stand up and crawl onto Liam's lap with my face inches from his, and I say, "Liam, the last thing I want to do is end this before we have even gotten a chance to really see what 'us' means. It would be easier and probably better for you if we did, but I am being selfish and not letting you go. The last few weeks have been an eye opener for me as well.

"I feel like this, us, is working, but just as I was patient with you when I gave you a second chance, I need you to be patient with me. Nothing is going on romantically between

Wren and me. He is involved in my life whether I like it or not. I have told him this and while he may not seem happy about it, he seems to respect my decision.

"Now, I have really missed you and would like to kiss you if that is okay." He gives me a small nod and I press my lips against his. In Liam's arms, I feel safe and comfortable, like this is where I belong.

I end the kiss and snuggle into him. With my head on his chest, I say, "I need a distraction from my life. Tell me about what I've missed these last three weeks with you."

I know Liam has questions. I basically disappeared for three weeks without any warning. Eventually, I will have to tell him something, but for now he is waiting until I bring it up.

Liam dives into the past few weeks talking about work and the house. I only catch about half of what he says while I feel his chest rumble under my head.

This is nice. I need more of this in my life.

After a nice afternoon just hanging out and drinking coffee with Liam, we drive back to The Academy. As we get closer, I start to become nervous about Wren.

He looked so sad before. Not angry, but sad. I know how to deal with angry Wren, not sad Wren.

As the front of The Academy comes into view, my stomach rolls and I feel as if I might puke. Where is this coming

Destiny

from?

Not wanting to worry Liam, I try to keep a brave face as I say goodbye and walk into The Academy. As soon as the door closes, the pain in my stomach becomes unbearable. Clutching it, I collapse onto the ground.

The cold tiles feel good on my warm cheek. Voices echo around me. The pain in my stomach increases as the nausea grows. I hate feeling weak, so I try to push it back. I need to get to my room and then I can fall apart where nobody is watching. As I try to move, my stomach rebels.

My throat burns as I empty my stomach on the entry room floor. Someone pulls my hair back and rubs my back.

There is yelling and feet pounding. I'm dizzy, floating.

A cup is shoved in my face. They want me to drink something, but I don't think my stomach will be able to keep it down. I struggle, not wanting to drink it.

My mouth is forced open. Cool liquid pours down my throat and hits my turbulent stomach. The soothing starts to happen slowly as the world around me comes back into focus.

Blinking a few times, I look around. A large crowd has gathered. Wren is holding me, and Edward is squatting down next to him with a bottle in his hand.

I look at them and ask, "What happened?"

Edward reaches forward and brushes hair out of my eyes. I know he is my father, but up until now, he has been trying to keep his distance. He looks at me with eyes that match mine and says, "Jamie, you were poisoned."

"Poisoned? But I was with Liam at Roberta's coffee shop all afternoon. How could I have been poisoned? Will Liam be okay?"

I reach for my phone. I need to call him and make sure he is okay.

Edward looks at me and asks, "How well do you know this Liam guy?"

Is he implying that Liam did this to me? He basically asked me to marry him today. Why would he try to kill me?

I frown at him. "Very well. He was my boss for three years and now he is my boyfriend." There are a few gasps from the crowd still circling us.

I get it, I slept with my boss. Why is that such a huge deal?

Behind me I feel Wren stiffen. And then it hits me. They don't care that he was my boss. It was the second part that shocked everyone. They all think I am with Wren. I will admit we have been acting like a couple since we got here, but why is there so much shock?

Edward breaks the awkward silence. "Well it is known that you frequent the shop, so someone may have added it when you weren't looking." He turns and barks at a few people in the crowd. "Tell everyone to stay away from the shop and inform Roberta what happened." Turning to another he says, "Start making more of the antidote just in case. If he got his hands on Moon Dust, we need to be prepared."

Moon dust? I feel lost.

If it was in what we were drinking, then that means Liam was poisoned, too. I try to stand up, but Wren holds onto me. I wrestle from his grip. "I need to go check on Liam. He could have been poisoned, too!"

I know he doesn't like the guy, but does he really want him to die?

Wren looks at me and says, "He is fine. Unless he is a wolf, the Moon Dust will have no effect on him. I've mentioned it before, Jamie, but you are in danger. The Eldest Brother is trying to kill you and he is running out of time, so his attempts are becoming bolder."

I'm too tired and confused to argue. "Okay, but I'm exhausted. Could you help me up to my room?"

As he helps me to my feet, I look down at the vomit that is on the floor. It's blood. I was vomiting blood.

Maybe it is time I started listening to Wren and accept that I am in danger.

Chapter 33:

Tired, sick, and lying in bed. Again. I stare up at the ceiling. This is getting old. I was finally starting to feel better and now I feel like I have to start all over again. Wren says that I got the antidote early enough, so it should pass quickly.

Why is the Eldest Brother trying to kill me?

I know there are things I am not being told and it is about time I figure them out. Today I will rest, but tomorrow I will hunt down answers. My plan is to start with Andre. He seems like he knows stuff and is young enough to bribe with candy.

My phone dings. **Liam** *Thanks for getting coffee with me, love you*

The love in the sign off hits me hard. He mentioned it in passing when I got into the car, but he never repeated it. Does he really love me or is this just a sign off?

Before I can reply, another text comes in. **Liam** *When can I see you again?*

A very good question, Liam. I have a feeling he would not

be welcome, and not just by Wren. Everyone in this building expects me to be with Wren. We are destined, why wouldn't we be together? Or at least that is what everyone here seems to think.

Hello, it's the twenty-first century and females have choices!

Why does everyone else have to be involved in my love life? Isn't finding out I have the wolf spirit enough for a girl for the week? Before I can venture any farther down the self-pity path, there's a knock on the door.

It's open, and I really don't feel like getting up, so I yell for them to come in.

Edward enters, taking me by surprise.

After our first interaction, when he told me he was my biological father, he has been keeping his distance.

He walks over and sits on the corner of the bed as I pull myself up to sit.

Looking at me, he asks, "How are you feeling?"

"I'm okay. My body was still not one hundred percent after the infection so it hit me hard, but I'm starting to feel better."

"That's good to hear. When I saw you crumple to the floor, I was worried we were too late. Moon Dust is like poison to us. It comes from the petals of a flower found deep in the forest and is very rare. Luckily, we always keep some antidote on hand just in case." He pauses and then continues. "One thing this did was confirm that you have the wolf spirit inside of you. If you didn't, it wouldn't have affected you. Why you haven't transformed, nobody seems to know."

I'm not sure how to talk to Edward. He is my father, but he is also a stranger. "Edward, I have no doubt that I have the wolf spirit in me. I can feel her inside of me. I always have, I just didn't realize what it was."

Edward, who is still looking uncomfortable says, "As soon as you are feeling better, we will help you figure out how to transform."

"Okay." Do I even want to transform?

Edward stands. "Jamie, I know you have no reason to listen to me, but I feel like I need to say this. How much do you know about Liam? From what Wren told me, the attacks started right before he came to town and have increased since he has been around. We know the description of the Eldest Brother from the legend, but nobody has seen him and knows what he actually looks like." He pauses as concern flashes across his face. "Maybe I am just getting ahead of myself, but it may be a good time to distance yourself from him."

I almost laugh at the insinuation. Liam. My *normal* option. Liam is the most normal person I know. Edward's wrong. Making something from nothing.

Sitting up a little straighter, I say, "I know you are just trying to watch out for me, but I am pretty good at doing it for myself. I have known Liam for over three years. He may not fit in here, but he isn't a wolf. He is my boyfriend, and I'd appreciate it if you didn't interrogate him. I will talk to him, see if I get anything from him hinting that he knows anything. He is the only normal I have left in my life. Don't ruin that."

I can tell he wants to say more but he stops himself. He walks toward the door, turning around right before he leaves. "Jamie, coming from your father and as the head minister of this school, you are not to leave these walls without a guard. It doesn't have to be Wren, but I don't want you going out alone. Not until you learn how to protect yourself."

Feeling like a scolded little girl, I send back a glare.

I hate being told what to do.

It's morning. I feel better and I am on a mission. Wren came in late, crawling into bed without a word. I know I should tell him we should sleep in separate beds, but I don't want to. I will soon, but for now I need the comfort.

He left before I woke up. I know he is upset. The moody Wren I first met has returned. I'll deal with him later. For now, I need answers.

With Wren being moody, I don't want to ask him. He has also been evading my questions. I can tell he is hiding something from me; my question is why?

Showered and dressed, I go in search of Andre. He may not know everything but it's a place to start. As I leave the room, I debate where to begin looking for him. It's too late for breakfast so the dining hall is out. The wing that classes take place in seems like the next best option.

The Academy is still very new to me, so if anyone asks what I am doing it will be easy to tell them I'm lost or that I'm just trying to get more acquainted with the building.

As I enter the wing, I find a room of older students. From what's on the board, it looks like they are learning some type of math. I always seem to forget that this is actually a school.

A little farther on, I hear grunting, people fighting. I hurry my pace to see if I can help. The wolf spirit seems to increase aggression in individuals, so fights are not an uncommon occurrence at The Academy.

As I round the corner, I find a gymnasium, where people are wrestling on mats.

My eyes zero in on Wren. He is fighting with one of the older students. His shirt is off, and he is glistening with sweat. And he's good, really good. I can tell he is holding back, but he is still clearly winning the fight.

A voice next to me snaps me out of my staring. "Sexy, isn't he?"

I look over to find the girl, Chloe, who I met before. I nod, mesmerized. I knew he could fight as a wolf, but it surprises me that they are training in human form.

Wren catches my eye and puts a pause to the fight. He grabs a shirt, wiping off his forehead before pulling it over his head. "Hey Jamie, how are you feeling?"

I blush, still thinking about how his ripped chest looked as he fought. "Better, like yesterday never happened."

"That's good to hear."

He looks over my shoulder and says in a warning tone, "Chloe, aren't you supposed to be in pre-calc right now?"

She mumbles something and scurries out of the room. Wren turns his attention back to me as I say, "She has a crush on you."

He smirks. "I know. She isn't exactly subtle about hiding it. I seem to be really good at attracting the ones I don't want and scaring away the ones I do."

Well, shit.

Thankfully, he changes the subject. "When are you going to join us? In the mornings, we train in human form and in the afternoon, we train in wolf form outside."

"Why do you train in human form? If you have claws, why would you not pull them out in a fight?"

He motions for me to follow him as he heads over to grab water. "It is important to be able to defend yourself at any time. I have experience so I can change very fast, but most can't, and it can put you in a precarious spot. Also, it's not always the best idea to change into a wolf. If you are in a place where people can see you, it's forbidden.

"But I am serious, Jamie, as soon as you are feeling up to it, I would like you to start training. And we need to see if we can get you to change. I would feel so much better if you were able to protect yourself. I can't always be there."

I do want to learn how to protect myself. I felt so helpless when that wolf was bounding towards me, and I hate that feeling.

I take the water Wren offers me and reply, "I would like that. This afternoon, I could come down. I don't know how long I will last, but I would like to start." Even if I never transform, I should at least know how to defend myself.

Wren heads back to the mats as I turn to leave. As I look over my shoulder, I see that his shirt is off again, and he is talking with the guys he was fighting with.

He put it on for me. He respects my decision and isn't trying to push me. Why can't he just be a jerk? This would all be easier if he was.

I push the door open to go in search of Andre. The Academy isn't that big, he must be here somewhere.

For the next two hours, I wander around The Academy. On the bright side I have a much better understanding of the layout, but all the walking has tired me out and I told Wren I would join him for training this afternoon.

Just as I am heading back to the room, I round a corner and find Andre. He is alone. Perfect.

I say his name and his head pops up. "Hello, Ms. Jamie, you are looking really nice today." Such a little charmer.

"Thanks, Andre, I was actually just looking for you. Have you eaten lunch yet?"

Hopefully my intuition will be right and he knows more than he should. I need answers.

Chapter 34:

What is the best way to get a young boy to talk about something he isn't supposed to talk about?

I know I can't just come out and ask. If it was that easy then I would have been able to just ask anyone and get the information, but they've all been evasive.

After we get food, we sit down at a table. It is still early so there aren't many people around, but I pick a table that is farther away in hopes that nobody will hear us.

All right Jamie, young boy, what do I talk about? "Hey Andre, so do you have any action figures?"

He gives me a look and then says, "Jamie, I'm ten. I don't have action figures. Those are for babies."

Well great, good job, Jamie. Now what do I say?

Luckily, he starts talking so I don't have to come up with something else.

"Video games and comics are my favorite. I love reading about superheroes. We are basically superheroes with the wolf spirit so it's cool. I'm not old enough to change yet, but I can feel him inside of me. Why haven't you changed yet? Everyone is talking about how you are different because you're a girl, but why should that matter?"

I shrug. "Andre, I wish I knew. All this is so new to me, I feel like a fish out of water. I'm finally feeling better, so we are hoping to work on me changing soon." If I decide to change. I haven't decided if I actually want to go down that road. This world seems so complicated, I want as little to do with it as possible.

"Well, I've heard adults talking; I can be very sneaky. Please don't tell on me," he says and I nod confirming his secret is safe with me. "If you don't change soon, it may mess everything up. There is supposed to be some ceremony during the spring solstice to bind you and Wren. And if it doesn't happen, we all die."

His words hit hard. *Bound to Wren. Must change. Die.*

Andre goes on about one of the comics he is reading while eating his pizza. I don't really hear what he is saying, and my appetite has disappeared.

Don't panic Jamie, this is coming from a ten-year-old. Not the world's most reliable source.

I knew they were hiding stuff, but if what Andre says is true, any chance at a regular life is lost. Isn't it?

Excusing myself, I walk out the balcony to call Liam. My normal.

It rings once and he picks up. "Hey beautiful, how are

you doing this morning?"

Terrible. Horrible. Confused. "Fine, what about you?"

"Good! It's been very productive. The last few weeks in general have been productive. It's amazing how much work you can get done when you are trying to distract yourself."

His words sink in. I know I have been putting him through a lot. I should let him go. But he is my normal and I don't want to lose that. "Well, I guess there is a bright side to any situation!"

My voice is a little too forced and he must be able to hear it, because he says, "Jamie, how are you really? You know you can talk to me about anything, right?"

Unfortunately, that is not true, unless I want you running for the hills.

Ignoring his question, I ask my own. "What are you up to? Want to do something?"

I hear some papers shuffle, then he answers, "Yeah, what did you have in mind? I can have my assistant move everything else for the day so we can spend it together."

I need a distraction. I don't care what we do as long as I am not here.

I ask, "How does lunch sound, and then we can go from there?"

"Sounds great. Are you ready now?"

"Yes. Perfect. Pick me up at The Academy?"

"Sounds good. Be there in ten."

With that, he hangs up and I hurry towards the front entrance. The sooner I leave this place behind, the better.

I run out and jump into Liam's car the second he pulls up, hoping to get out of here before anyone can stop me. I need space, room to breathe, and the walls of The Academy feel as if they are closing in on me.

Seeing my haste, Liam pulls out quickly. He waits until we are a little way down the road before pulling over to the side, cutting the engine, and turning to me.

"Jamie, what's up? You are starting to scare me. You need to give me something."

I can't give him everything, but he deserves an explanation. "Okay, but it is going to sound crazy. Bear with me until I am done."

Trying to decide what to say, I pause a moment. It would be really nice to have some outside perspective on this. I take a deep breath.

"So last week, when I disappeared, I was very sick. It turns out I have this weird genetic thing that caused me to get fevers and sleep for a long time. That is why I was at The Academy, not the hospital. It's because they know how to deal with it. I kept trying to ignore it, but it is becoming more and more difficult.

"I just want to have a simple and traditional life, but the more I learn, the less I think that will be possible. Also, to top it all off, I just learned my mom had an affair with the headmaster of The Academy. So, my dad is not my biological dad.

"I really care about you, but I can't seem to fully trust you yet. You have been great since you reached out, but I can't help but wonder what caused your change in attitude. Nothing is simple and I feel like I just can't handle much more."

After I say the last words, I pull my knees into my chest and begin to cry. I hate crying, especially in front of other people. But I can't hold it in any longer. Why did this have to happen to me? Why does this have to be my destiny?

Liam puts his hand on mine, slowly stroking it with his fingers.

Neither of us is in the mood to go out, so Liam drives us back to his house. I'm still so upset, the second we walk inside, I crawl on the couch, pulling a fuzzy blanket around myself.

From the other room, I hear Liam on the phone, ordering pizza. He is being patient, waiting for me. I'll discuss it in a little while, but for now I want to forget it.

My phone rings in my pocket and dings with texts, and I know my disappearance has been noted. I'm right down the street, inside Liam's house. What is going to hurt me here?

I turn my phone to silent and close my eyes. Before I know it, I drift off.

―•―

"She doesn't want to see you."
"I don't care what she wants. I'm here to make sure she

is safe."

"Why wouldn't she be safe? She told me about her illness and about her father. I think she just needs a little time to process everything."

"She told *you* about that?"

"Yes."

"Tell her to call me back when she wakes up."

I hear the crunch of gravel as a new car arrives. Then footsteps, followed by, "Pizza delivery for Liam."

Liam responds, "That would be for me, thank you. Keep the change." More crunching of gravel and then the sound of tires pulling out.

Liam speaks again. "Wren, I don't know what all is going on with her, but she came to me for comfort and to get away from The Academy. She needs time. I will keep an eye on her. I love her; I won't let anything bad happen to her."

There are those words again, *I love you.*

He really does care about me.

I must drift off because I wake to a hand, smoothing my hair. My eyes open slowly. Liam is squatting in front of me.

"Hey babe, how are you feeling? The pizza's here if you would like some."

The argument I heard comes back. "Is Wren here?"

He shakes his head. "He stopped by to check on you, but he is gone now. I told him you needed some time. I thought he was going to rip my head off at first."

I knew he would be angry that I left, but I just needed to

get away. Andre's words keep circling in my brain, *bind me to Wren, if I don't change, I will die.*

I need to talk to Edward and get answers. And I will. Just not tonight. Tonight, I am going to enjoy a ordinary night on the couch with my boyfriend, eating pizza, and watching a movie.

"Yes, pizza sounds nice. Could we eat it in here and watch a movie?"

"Yeah, that sounds great. Let me grab the box and some drinks."

As he walks away, I settle in, determined to have a nice night. As I am flipping through channels, Liam comes back with the pizza. He sets it down on the ottoman and hands me a plate. "So, what are we watching?"

"I saw *Pitch Perfect* just started. You okay with that?"

"I'm okay with whatever you want. I just like being here with you."

This moment is so normal, so perfect. I wish I could just freeze time.

Chapter 35:

My calm is destroyed as I open my eyes to the sound of my phone ringing. I thought I'd turned it to silent.

The bed is so warm and cozy, I roll over and groan, hoping to enjoy the peace for a few more minutes.

The ringing starts again, and I know my time is up. Throwing the blankets off, I put my feet on the cold ground and search for the ringing phone.

Liam isn't in bed, but I didn't expect him to be. From the way the light filters in the window, I would guess it is probably almost noon. Grabbing the throw from the end of the bed, I wrap it around my shoulders.

Since I was scratched, I never seem to feel warm. I felt like I was burning alive for weeks, so it makes sense that my temperature gauge is a little off.

Going to the couch where we watched all three *Pitch Perfect* movies yesterday, I locate my phone. It's dead. Then I hear the ringing again and follow it to the kitchen.

It's coming from the landline on the counter. I pick it up and answer.

"Hello?" There is heavy breathing on the other end of the line and I instantly know it's Wren.

How did he get this number?

"Jamie, thank god. I was so worried. I have been calling your phone all morning and you didn't answer."

I decide to not tell him it is dead. Let him think I was ignoring him. He deserves it for thinking I can just belong to him so easily.

"Wren, how did you get this number?"

"That's not important. What's important is that you are safe."

"Yes, Wren, I am fine. I was sleeping. You just woke me up."

"There was another attack, Jamie. On the guys patrolling the forest around Liam's house last night. They were able to hold him off with only minor injuries, but I haven't been able to get ahold of you or Liam. I promised him I would give you space, but I needed to make sure you were okay."

Attacked? Guarding the house? Is my selfishness putting others in danger?

"Physically, I'm fine, Wren, but mentally, not so much. I need to know what is going on. The whole story. Not just the abridged, we-don't-want-to-hurt-her-feelings story. I need all the gory details."

He lets out a frustrated sigh. "No, Jamie. I can't. Not

yet."

"Then I'm not coming back to you."

He growls, "You are in danger; serious danger and you can't just go running off. You scared the shit out of me yesterday. What were you thinking? Wait, don't answer that. You weren't thinking, which is the problem. I know all of this is a lot and it's new, I get it, but if I can't trust you to stay where you are safe then we will lock you up."

He wouldn't dare. I know I have been pushing the boundaries, but that's a little much, even for Wren.

"I want to talk to Edward. After I do that, we can discuss what will happen next."

"Fine. I will be there in an hour." Before I can say anything else, he hangs up. As frustrated as ever, I slump into one of the kitchen chairs.

Maybe once I know all the information, they will stop treating me like a child. *Jamie, if you want them to stop treating you like a child, stop acting like one.*

Liam walks into the kitchen. "Hey babe, how do you feel this morning?"

I was feeling better until I talked to Wren. Even when I agree with him, I can't help from letting him under my skin.

I reply, "Better. Wren will be here in an hour. It's time I talked to Edward and get all the details. Thank you for being so supportive last night. It meant the world to me."

"Of course, whatever you need. Are you hungry?"

"Yeah. I need to go take a shower really quick and then

I'll help you make something." Liam may be great at a lot of things, but cooking is not one of them.

Showered and dressed in some of the clothes that I left here the last time I stayed, I walk into the kitchen to the smell of bacon and coffee. On cue, my stomach rumbles.

I find Liam at the stove, flipping bacon, and a plate of croissants on the table. He hands me a coffee and I take a sip. It's exactly the way I like it.

Setting the mug down, I walk up and hug him from behind. He is tall, so my face only comes to between his shoulder blades. "Liam, this smells amazing. I didn't know you knew how to cook."

He spins around and smiles down at me. "There are a lot of things you don't know about me. Plus, I wouldn't go that far. I can cook bacon and pasta, but that's about it."

I grab my coffee and sit in one of the chairs on the island to watch Liam cook.

When I was younger, I always fantasized about relationships; imagining fancy dinners, gifts, huge houses with white picket fences. But at this moment, I could care less about any of that. What is important is this connection. This domestic activity together. The simplicity of making and eating breakfast together.

As Liam pulls the bacon off the stove and comes to sit next to me, I can't help but smile. This is nice. Really nice.

But too soon, there's a knock on the door, dragging me out of my normal life. Wren is here to pop my perfect bubble.

I kiss Liam goodbye, desperately hoping I will see him again. I know this conversation is going to change everything.

I walk with Wren to his Jeep. We drive in silence and I feel as if I am going to my execution.

As he marches me through the doorway of The Academy, I feel the pressure return to my shoulders. I didn't realize the effect this building had on me until I was out of it.

I follow Wren to Edward's office, feeling as if every person I pass has their eyes on me. Is this what it feels like being a celebrity? Never being able to have any private life? Always being on display?

Relief settles in when we enter an empty hallway. About halfway down, Wren opens a door and motions me inside an office. The walls are lined with bookshelves towering up to the vaulted ceiling. Everything is dark wood and manly. I feel as if I have just walked into an old library.

A large desk dominates the room with an arched window behind it. Edward is standing in the light of the window, black against white. He turns and motions me to a chair, and I sit. "Hello darling, thank you for coming by. I know this whole situation has been difficult and for that I am sorry, but what I am about to tell you isn't going to make it better. Which is why we have been waiting to tell you. We wanted to give you some time to get used to who you are." He pauses. "Would you like something to drink before we get started?"

I nod yes, knowing I am going to need something strong to get through this.

Edward goes to a bar in the corner of the room and pours three glasses of amber liquid. Handing one to each of us, he motions to the couches near the fireplace.

Under different circumstances, I would love this room. Curled up on this couch in front of the fire with a book on a snowy day seems perfect.

Wren sits down and I choose the chair across from him so that he won't be able to touch me. I don't need anything distracting me.

I take a sip, and the liquid burns down my throat and settles into my stomach. Edward paces in front of the fireplace.

"Wren filled you in on how the Wolf Warriors came to be and the prophecy a few weeks ago. But a few years after the lady that lived in the woods moved into town, she had another vision. Due to the actions of the eldest brother, the wolf spirits became angry. This was a gift and it was never intended to be used in the way he was using it. He had tainted the spirit inside him and they wanted him gone.

"The second prophecy stated, *Magic is a gift. When used correctly, it is incredible, but once tainted, it runs black. On the spring solstice of the white wolf's 26th year, she is to be bound to her lover. This union will destroy the evil. He will lurk where you least expect it, don't lose sight of the end. Death will follow, good or evil, if the choice is not made.*

"Jamie, if I am correct, your birthday is in a month, so the spring solstice of next year is the one referenced in the prophecy. You have been destined to bind yourself to Wren since before you were born. This will bring the two wolf spirit lines together and cause those who have become tainted to escape from their captors.

"If the ceremony happens, the eldest brother and all the evil he created will die. If it doesn't, both our line and Wren's line will die, as they will wipe out all those who house the wolf spirit. It wasn't used as they intended, and this is their way of gaining a fresh slate, for lack of a better term."

Finally, he stops and both of them stare at me to see my reaction.

How is anyone supposed to react to something like this?

If I am not bound to Wren, then I die. What kind of choice is this? I have never been someone who likes being told what to do. Maybe that was the wolf spirit inside me rebelling since she knew I didn't have a choice.

Maybe I still do?

"You said I had to be bound to Wren. I'm not going to let everyone die, so of course I will, but that doesn't mean I have to be part of this world, right? Could we do the ceremony and I go on with my life like nothing has changed? I would have the traditional life that I want."

I look up and see Wren's face. The guilt instantly hits me. He looks devastated.

Edward takes a drink then looks at me. "Jamie, I know you were raised by your mother and were taught to have a strong will. While that is something I admire about you, there is something called duty, and this is your duty to your people.

You have had 25 years to live your life as you please. And live you have; I have always kept track of you and your activities."

Blush creeps into my cheeks and I wonder how much he knows about Liam. How he knows, I'm not sure, but I have a feeling nothing happens without him being aware. I have seen a very calm, nice side of Edward, but I have a feeling he is in charge for a reason.

"Jamie, all I am asking is you give it a try. We are not evil and forcing you to your death. This community is very close and enjoyable. I know you have never handled change well, but please, for me, for Wren, for yourself. Give all this a chance." With his hands, he motions to The Academy.

I feel guilty again. I have been trying so hard to rebel, maybe I haven't given anything a chance. Looking at Edward and then Wren, I say, "Fine. I promise to try, but can you do something for me in exchange?"

Edward nods.

"Please look into the details of the prophecy. As open minded as I am trying to be, I just hate the idea of needing to be bound to someone."

"We have been doing research on it for years, but I will. All right, I must get downstairs to teach a class. You guys are free to stay here as long as you would like."

There is a click as the door closes behind Edward. I know he left us alone on purpose. We need to talk, and I guess now is as good of time as any.

Wren starts to speak and I stop him. "Wren, please let me

say this and then you can talk. I know it feels like all my hesitance is directed at you but it's not. I like you and I think we have become good friends. And maybe we will become more than that, but I don't want some mystical prophecy to be the reason why. That is no reason to be in a relationship.

"It is almost September which means we have seven months until the spring solstice. For just a little while, let's try to push the prophecy aside and be friends. Do things friends would do? I feel like half the time we are together, we are arguing or you are yelling at me.

"Let's start over, okay? Hello, my name is Jamie. Recently, my whole life got turned upside down and I am handling it as best as I can."

I look over at Wren and he is smirking. It is always a shock to see his face hold an expression other than his typical scowl.

"Hello, Jamie, my name is Wren. My life has been crazy since birth, so sometimes I forget how it would seem to someone who is new to this world. You appear nice and I think I would enjoy being your friend. I can't promise to not get angry at you, but I will try as long as you actually follow precautions to keep yourself safe."

I smile back at him. We can do this; I can do this. Edward is right, I never gave it a chance. I have been fighting against it since day one, even if I didn't realize what I was fighting against at the time.

For the next hour, I talk with Wren and he answers all the questions I have. I ask him about the possibility of me never changing, and while he looks worried, he tells me it is my choice. Then he explains the feeling of running through the forest with the breeze on your face. I tell him I will think about it, but for the time being, I want to learn how to fight and protect myself without claws.

We decide to keep the conversation going over lunch. Wren opens the door for me, and not paying attention, I walk straight into someone.

I look up and freeze.

Green eyes. Red hair. He is older than I remember, but it's been fifteen years.

My brother. He is here and he is alive.

"Jacob," his name comes out as barely a whisper.

"Hey, Jamie."

What the fuck is going on?

THE END

Book 2:
Journey **Avaible July 2021, Preorder now!**

More by D. D. Larsen:
Perfect. (Perfect Series)
Imperfect. (Perfect Series)

Follow me on Social Media:
Instagram: @d.d.larsen
Facebook: @d.d.larsenauthor
Facebook Reader Group: D's Reading Divas
Twitter: @ddlarsen2

Thank you, lovelies!
Xoxo, D.

Made in the USA
Monee, IL
16 September 2021